Spin Control

How Not to Spend Your Senior Year
BY CAMERON DOKEY

Royally Jacked
BY NIKI BURNHAM

Ripped at the Seams
BY NANCY KRULIK

Cupidity
BY CAROLINE GOODE

South Beach Sizzle
BY SUZANNE WEYN AND DIANA GONZALEZ
COMING SOON

Spin Control

NIKI BURNHAM

Simon Pulse
New York London Toronto Sydney

This book is a work of fiction. Any references to historical events, real people, or real locales are used fictitiously. Other names, characters, places, and incidents are the product of the author's imagination, and any resemblance to actual events or locales or persons, living or dead, is entirely coincidental.

〰 SIMON PULSE
An imprint of Simon & Schuster
Children's Publishing Division
1230 Avenue of the Americas, New York, NY 10020
Copyright © 2005 by Nicole Burnham

SIMON PULSE and colophon are registered trademarks of Simon & Schuster, Inc.

Designed by Ann Zeak
The text of this book was set in Garamond 3.

Manufactured in the United States of America
First Simon Pulse edition January 2005

10 9 8 7 6 5 4 3 2 1
Library of Congress Control Number 2004108250
ISBN 0-689-86669-0

For Doug,
for encouraging me to spin

Spin Control

One

Exactly six weeks, five days, and nine hours ago, my mother ruined my life. And even worse, because of her, I am missing a damned good party.

Right this second, I should be over at my best friend Christie Toleski's house, getting ready to watch hotties like Heath Ledger walk the red carpet at the Golden Globes. My friends Natalie Monschroeder and Julia (aka Jules) Jackson are already there, undoubtedly noshing on popcorn, watching Joan Rivers on television and discussing the plasticity of Joan's face while she kisses and disses the celebs and their clothes—or lack thereof.

When Christie's parents aren't in the room, they're also probably talking about how far Christie and her boyfriend, Jeremy Astin, went on their last date, how far she actually wants to go, and how all of them are sooooo sure David Anderson (who I've been crushing on since kindergarten) is finally interested in me.

But no. They're doing all that without me. I know because they IM'ed me about half an hour ago to rub it in.

Unfortunately, my failure to attend this year's let's-make-fun-of-celebrities Golden Globes party (not to be confused with our annual let's-make-fun-of-celebrities Oscar, Grammy, and Emmy parties) is because, thanks to my mother, my parents are getting a divorce and I had to move with my dad to Schwerinborg a month ago.

Yes, Schwerinborg's a real country, and yes, my friends all refer to it as Smorgasbord, even though the people here aren't even Scandinavian. The Schwerinborgians—or Schwerinborgers or whatever they're called—speak German. And we're south of Germany, not north. Not that any of my friends care where it is, other than the fact that it's very, very far from Virginia.

So why not live with my mother? After all, she has a nice apartment back in Virginia, where all the important awards shows are carried live. And even though the location of Mom's new place means I'd have to go to Lake Braddock High School instead of to Vienna West, where I've been going, I could still see my friends on a regular basis.

Hmmmm . . . how about because Mom's new apartment is also home to Mom's new GIRLFRIEND?

Yep, girlfriend. A super-organized, yoga-twisting, vegan Weight Watchers—devotee girlfriend named Gabrielle, who is, no kidding, a decade younger than my mother. And no, Gabrielle isn't a girlfriend like Christie, Natalie, and Jules are my girlfriends.

Gabrielle is THAT kind of girlfriend.

I haven't even had the guts to tell *my* girlfriends about her, and it doesn't take a psychology degree to guess why. It's the kind of thing that takes you a while to work up to telling someone, even your best friends. Telling them about my parents' divorce—and that I was moving to Europe with Dad—was bad enough. Popping out with, "Oh, and by the way, my mom—the woman who took us all out for manicures and facials before homecoming and has definitely seen all of you naked at one time or another when we've gone clothes shopping—yeah, well, she's decided she's gay!" wouldn't have gone over with them very well.

I know they say they don't care whether a person is gay, and I've never heard them say one derogatory word about anyone's sexual preferences, but I'm not quite sure I want to test their beliefs yet.

And it's not that *I'm* a homophobe. Seriously. I know a couple of gay kids at school, and they're totally cool. But this is different. This is MY MOTHER.

It's like the mom I knew disappeared one day and now there's another person inhabiting Mom's body. That's the really hard part. Not the what-is-she-doing-with-that-woman? part. It's that I have to wonder if she's lied to me about who she is my entire freaking life.

You'd think I'd want to find the highest turret—well, if it had turrets—of Schwerinborg's royal palace and toss myself off of it.

But no. I'm not even close to suicidal right now, even though I'm sure Heath Ledger and Hugh Jackman and about a hundred other hot actors look completely droolworthy walking the red carpet in their Armani tuxes and I'm missing it. (Thankyouverymuch, Mom.)

It's because Schwerinborg is completely incredible. I mean, there are definite downsides, like the fact they use mayo on their French fries, that the weather is misty and depressing all winter long, and that I can't watch the Golden Globes live. (Which, come to think of it, makes absolutely no sense—the awards are given by the Hollywood Foreign Press, and if anything's foreign to Hollywood, it's gotta be Schwerinborg.)

It's because I have a BOYFRIEND.

I have a boyfriend who looks like Colin Farrell, only better. More of a hottie, less of a male slut.

I have a boyfriend named Georg

Jacques von Ederhollern, *and he is a freakin'*
PRINCE.

Yep. I, Valerie Winslow, a totally boring, non-cheerleader, non-athletic, non-popular sophomore redheaded nobody from Vienna, Virginia, have officially hooked up with a European prince. A prince who knows how to kiss in the most knock-me-on-my-ass way, and who is formal and polite and looks beyond hot in a tux, but who also knows how to kick back and be cool and totally un-prince-like when we're alone, if you catch my drift.

And you wanna know a secret? Even though it's the dead of winter and he's always in sweaters and jackets, I've discovered that he has these amazing arms.

Ever see Hugh Jackman in *X-Men?* Or when he has his shirt off in *Someone Like You?* Yeah. THOSE arms.

Okay, Georg's almost seventeen, so he's not quite Jackman caliber yet, and he's a lot more lean and wiry than Hugh Jackman, but he's headed in that direction. His arms are totally ripped and solid—the kind that other guys refer to as guns. A girl could be about to go off a cliff, grab on to those biceps just as her footing slips, and not worry for even a second she's going to fall, you know?

Yes, I know that girls probably go for Hugh Jackman—and Heath Ledger and Colin Farrell, for that matter—because of their accents as much as their arms or other, um, physical attributes. But if his name alone doesn't make it clear, Georg *also* has an accent, and it's pretty damned sexy. Better than Hugh's, Heath's, or Colin's, even. (However, I will admit that if someone had told me a year ago that listening to a guy speak with a deep, German accent would make me get all gooey inside, I'd have thought they needed some serious therapy.)

But you see, the thing that makes Georg an even better boyfriend than Hugh Jackman could ever be is . . . HUGH JACKMAN DOES NOT HAVE A CROWN! He does not have staff members who polish his shoes before school or ask him if he'd like a Coke or finger sandwiches while he's studying Trig in the palace library. Georg does. And he's not the least bit egotistical about any of those things. In fact, it makes him blush if you mention it. He gets this little pink glow right along his cheekbones, and then he tries to hide his face so you can't see. It's totally cute.

Also, Georg does not care that my mother is a lesbian. He actually tells me I should try to be more understanding of her, and at the same time, he totally gets that while I really do love her, I'm completely ticked off at her for what she did to me and Dad.

Is that love, or what? You don't find that with just any guy. The arms, the accent, and even the crown are simply bonus material. He likes me for me, and David Anderson never did.

Well, unless you believe my friends, who I think keep telling me David likes me to try to make me feel better about the whole divorce thing.

Ha.

Wait until they hear about my prince. Or better yet, wait until I put them on the phone with him so they can hear his accent.

So right now *I'm* on the phone with Georg, and I can hardly follow what he's saying, because I'm so hung up on how he's saying it. All rich and Euro-like, but thankfully without even a hint of that thick nasal sound that Arnold Schwarzenegger makes. Georg's voice is way more smooth and seductive. And it's making me wish he would hurry up and get over here so I can grab him and kiss him the way he kissed me day before yesterday, when we went to this dinner-party-reception-formal thing his father was hosting for the British prime minister here at the palace, then ditched for a while to go make out in the garden. It was icy out there, and all the plants were that generic shade of gray-green that plants get in the middle of January, but between the kissing and him whispering to me in that fabulous accent, I was totally warm. It was our second kiss, but the first serious one, and this time we both knew there'd be more. Lots and lots more.

I can't think about anything else *but* kissing Georg.

"Valerie. Are you still listening to me?"

I sit up on my bed and try to focus. It's difficult, though, when my room is maybe only five degrees warmer than the garden was and Georg isn't here to keep me toasty.

My dad and I live in the royal palace in Schwerinborg because he's the new protocol chief to the royal family—meaning he works for Georg's dad, Prince Manfred—who rules the country—and Georg's mom, Princess Claudia. He advises them on things like the proper way to address everyone from visiting Buddhist monks to the queen of England, and warns them about the fact that when they visit Egypt, they might get served pigeon but that it's perfectly safe to eat.

It's a totally whacked thing to do for a living, but since it got me a behind-the-scenes tour of the White House (which is where my dad did his protocol thing until the überconservative, up-for-re-election president discovered Dad had married a lesbian) and it's the reason I met Georg and have gotten to hang out with him despite the fact I'm your average American fifteen-year-old, I'm not going to make even one crack about it.

On the other hand, while it might sound cool to actually *live* in a real palace,

I'd much rather the royal couple hadn't offered us their, uh, hospitality. Other than the fact that Georg is under the same roof, it pretty much sucks. Our very ritzy-sounding "palace apartment"——which is actually only three small rooms and a kitchen——is always so cold I have to wear double layers of socks, and it has the decor of a circa-1970s, never-been-renovated Holiday Inn. Probably because we're in a 150-year-old section of the palace that hasn't been renovated since, well, the 1970s. We'd have been better off living a couple blocks away, in a nice little walk-up.

Preferably one with heat.

"Yeah, I'm listening," I say to Georg as I stare at my tiny, ancient bedroom window and wonder how much cold air is leaking in from outside. "You said you had two assists and a goal at the scrimmage yesterday. But I wish you'd just come over. I can follow soccer talk much better in person."

I'm totally kidding because we both know it's way too late, but still. Does he think a five-minute walk from one side of the palace——the beautiful, *warm,* renovated side, where his family lives——over to the other side, where my apartment is, would kill him? I mean, the guy's an incredible soccer player, so you know his legs work just fine.

They're very nice legs. All tight and muscular and—

Whoa.

This thought zaps my brain back to reality. I have it bad for him. Way bad. I can't stop thinking about his various body parts, and we went out—officially—for the first time, what, Friday night, and it's only Sunday?!

Maybe I'm wigged out because this is the first time I've ever had a real boyfriend (since I don't count Jason Barrows, who everyone thought I was going out with because he kissed me on a dare in seventh grade. Puh-leeze.). Maybe it's because Georg's a prince, and no matter where he goes, he always has this prince-like aura around him.

But even so, this is not good because Georg and I are trying to keep things low-key, or at least make it look that way for the time being.

Given the way my synapses are firing

right now, though, if Georg and I get within fifty feet of each other, I'm going to be all over him. On top of it making me look totally desperate, which would be bad because Georg has no idea I'm a little, um, inexperienced, it would blow the whole low-key thing out of the water.

"I know you're kidding, but if I thought we could get away with it, I would," Georg tells me. "But it's nearly midnight. My father said the fund-raiser would be over around one a.m., which means everyone will be back soon. Until your father's not suspicious about the cig-arettes anymore . . . well, we have to be careful."

"I know." I twist one of my sheets into a little whorl with my fingers, then glance at the bedside alarm clock. "I still can't believe we got busted."

We weren't even smoking them when my dad walked in on us Friday night, and we weren't going to. Really. Georg was just showing me where he keeps an emergency stash, behind the paper towel holder in the handicapped stall of the men's restroom that's below the palace ballroom. He'd even hidden them back away before my dad came in, but they'd fallen on the floor.

Major oops.

I must be pretty desperate, though, because I add, this time only half-joking, "I still think you'd be okay, if you really wanted to come over. Now that Dad's had a day to chill, he's beginning to understand that I wasn't trying to corrupt you with cigarettes."

"And get him fired."

"Exactly." Europeans are pretty lax about smoking—just not when it comes to their royalty. Apparently, Georg getting caught with cigarettes—say, by the press or something—would be a pretty big deal.

I pull the covers up over my shoulders like a cape, then cradle the phone a little closer to my ear. "I told him they were on the sink when we got there, and one of us must have accidentally knocked them off when we were, ah, *talking* in there."

If it's possible to hear someone smile over the phone, I can hear it. "Well, that's good news, at least. So he seems to think it's okay if we're going out?"

"Hey, all we're doing is engaging in a

little soccer talk, right? Nothing that will jeopardize your reputation as the next leader of Schwerinborg."

He laughs, but it dies out pretty quickly, which means he's thinking about something serious. "Well, that's what I was getting to. Some of the guys were talking yesterday after we got out of practice."

"Yeah?"

"Well, remember how Ulrike's dad was at the dinner on Friday night? He must have mentioned seeing us together to Ulrike, because the guys were asking me about it."

Uh-oh. I know exactly where this is going. Ulrike is this really nice girl at my new high school who's the president of everything. One of those girls with white-blond hair and a perfect Crest smile, and who I usually write off based on her looks alone, because 99 percent of girls who look like Ulrike are just heinous. Snobby and mean and they think they're God's gift to the world. But Ulrike's actually really smart and friendly—and not just to other beautiful people, but to everyone.

On the other hand, Ulrike has this

equally beautiful friend, Steffi, who's the world's biggest bitch. One of those fake, manipulative people no one—especially naive, trusting types like Ulrike—ever *get* until it's way too late.

"Let me guess—"

"Yeah, I'm pretty sure Steffi already knows we're together." Georg sounds irritated by Steffi's mere existence as he talks. "If not, she'll know soon. Thought we should figure out how we're going to handle it when she asks us about it."

Great. It's not that I really care if she knows. Maybe it'll knock her down a peg to realize that just because she's tiny and brunette and popular, she can't get any guy she wants. Like Georg.

But chances are, rather than just acting like a normal person with hurt feelings when she hears that the object of her crush has a new girlfriend, she'll get totally ticked off, meaning she'll be more aggressive than usual about giving me backhanded compliments when everyone's around . . . making offhand comments about how I must have some wonderful hidden traits if Georg is willing to take the time to introduce me around the school when he's such a busy person.

As if whatever good traits I might have aren't obvious, or as if Georg is doing me this huge favor because I'm clearly not good enough to be around him.

Steffi's like that. You can't really pick apart anything she says as being nasty and call her on it, because she says it in this fakey-nice, syrupy way. But I know she wants me to get the message, especially because she makes genuinely nasty little remarks to me under her breath when she knows no one else can hear—she's so quiet with it, I can barely hear her.

So I say to Georg, "Well, you know how I usually deal with Steffi. I ignore her. But what do you think?"

As much as I'd like to rant to Georg about what Steffi can do with her opinions, I don't, because I know it'll only make me sound like a whiner. Georg tries to be nice to Steffi—since he's a prince, he's stuck trying to be nice to everyone or else risk his family's good reputation, which really sucks if you think about it—but he's the one guy in school who sees right through her.

And I love that about him. We have this funky-cool connection, where we just look at each other and *know* we both see the world the same way. As deranged as it is, the fact we both get Steffi and her little games—when no one else does—just makes our connection that much stronger.

"Well, I figure we have three choices—assuming she actually asks us what's going on. First, we can play dumb. Second choice, we act like it's no big thing, and say we were just at the reception together because we both live under the same roof and thought it'd be fun."

"And third?"

"We come clean, and who cares if Steffi knows we've hooked up." I can hear the smile in his voice again. "And that's the fun option, because it means if I feel like kissing you between classes, I can, which definitely has its appeal."

"So what do you want to do?" No way am I making this call. I like option three, for the same reason Georg does. Frankly, a quickie make-out session with Georg—of course where Steffi can see—would totally strengthen my ability to deal with her and all her crap. But Georg knows Ulrike, Steffi, their friend Maya, and all the rest of the kids at school way better than I do. So I figure he's the one who should decide.

"I'd prefer to be honest about it." His voice has that tone that makes it sound like a *but* is coming, and it does. "But the more I think about it, the more I think it wouldn't be smart."

I make a face at the wall. Ooo-kay. Georg was the one who said he didn't care if Ulrike's father saw us dancing together, or who knew about us. And now he does?

"So I shouldn't say anything around school?" I guess it would pretty much be the gossip of the week if we confirmed it to anyone. But why should he care?

Then I realize that I'm the hypocrite of the century. I'm freaked about him not wanting to tell his friends, even though I still haven't told my friends about him— let alone about my mother and everything else. And they're thousands of miles away.

I'm about to apologize, and say we can do whatever he wants, when he says, "School isn't really the problem. It's the people outside of school. Okay, Steffi's a problem, but it's not her attitude around school that worries me. It's who else she talks to."

He gets quiet a second, and the light-bulb turns on in my head. Now I get it. Tabloids.

There's this one reporter assigned to Georg who walks about twenty yards behind him on the way to school a couple times a week. The poor guy's probably the bottom of the food chain at *Majesty* magazine. There really isn't much to report about Georg—his parents crack down on him hard, so he really can't get in any trouble, he doesn't go out partying; and I'm willing to bet most of the world's population couldn't find Schwerinborg on a map, let alone identify its prince. Not like they could Prince William or Prince Harry.

But still, Georg is always careful, so that most of the reports this guy files are about fairly innocuous things, like last week's story, "Teen Prince Risking His Smile," which ran alongside a snapshot of Georg ducking out of a coffeehouse on his way to school, but mostly talked about how if you drink coffee or tea for years and years, your teeth can get stained.

"Valerie, I don't want you to think I'm embarrassed to be with you, or that I don't want anyone to know—"

"Hey, no problem. Really." And I mean it. I don't exactly want to be on the front of some trashy rag either. I'm beginning to realize that keeping things low-key goes with the dating-a-prince territory, even if you weren't almost caught smoking.

"You know how I feel about you. It's just that—"

He sounds so concerned about it, I can't help but laugh. I know I shouldn't—my dad would probably tell me it's against some very important rule of protocol—but I can't help it. "I told you, no problem."

He's quiet for a sec, then says, "If I hurry, I can be over there in five minutes, stay for maybe twenty, then get back before my parents are home from the fund-raiser. I just need to watch the clock so I have a five-to-ten-minute cushion."

"And what if we get caught?"

"Have your Chemistry book out, maybe?"

This time I'm really laughing, because my dad knows—and so does Georg—that I'm a total geek, and there's no way I'd put my Chem homework off until midnight Sunday. I can hardly stand to have homework that's not done by Saturday at noon.

Is it any mystery why I haven't had a boyfriend before?

His voice is low and completely hot as he tells me, "I'll be there in five minutes, like it or not."

"Not!"

Exactly four minutes and thirty-two seconds later, there's a knock at my apartment door. And I definitely like it.

To: Val@realmail.sg.com
From: ChristieT@viennawest.edu
Subject: Armor Girls

Heya, Val Pal!
Can I just say I'm totally bummed you missed the GGs last night? Joan was in fine form, and Melissa Rivers was wearing a dress that was totally see-through when she stood under the lights. They kept having to cut away from her and back to Joan, which was hysterical. You'd have

made tons of jokes about Melissa wanting to show off her boob job.

So—here's the hottie report: My dearest Orlando Bloom looked devastating, even though he was there with this snotty little French actress. (I was heartbroken he didn't think to stop in Virginia and ask me to be his GG date, but don't tell Jeremy.) And Heath Ledger made *me* drool, he looked so good, even though you know I usually don't go for him. BTW, Jules told me about your Armor Girl theory—the whole thing about *A Knight's Tale,* the movie where Heath falls for this totally shallow rich-girl-princess type and ignores the girl who makes his armor. Jules claims that you think you're only an Armor Girl to David Anderson's knight, and that he's only interested in you until he can find a Shallow Princess.

You are WRONG.

Tonight sucks for me, but you will be home tomorrow night, so I can FINALLY talk to you on the phone, right? I was nice to my cousins for an entire week so my mom would let me call you, and you haven't been there. Now you MUST be. Because I have actually talked to David about you, and you are so not an Armor Girl.

DO YOU GET IT YET?! YOU ARE THE PRINCESS.

I'm tired of dropping hints about this, which

is why I'm cyber-yelling. You said you could change your mind and live with your mom if you wanted. I think you should. (I promise I will forgive you for going to Smorgasbord.) Natalie and Jules think you should come home too.

How often do all three of us agree on something? Seriously. Think about it. I know you told Jules that you thought David could never really like you for you—but you are so, so wrong. David is perfect for you. AND HE WANTS YOU.

Hugs and miss you and etc.,
Christie

P.S. So what is this "unbelievable dirt" you told me about in your e-mail on Friday night? PLEASE tell me you haven't met someone. And if you did, get over him. He's not David.

To: Val@realmail.sg.com
From: CoolJule@viennawest.edu
Subject: You and your potential ass-kicking

Yo, Valerie!

Five very important things. Are you paying attention?? GOOD.

Number 1: Okay, I will acknowledge,

after seeing him at last night's Golden Globes, that Heath Ledger is hot.

Number 2: You're still wrong about the Armor Girl thing. I told Natalie and Christie about it when we saw Heath on TV, and they totally agree with me that you're the princess, NOT the Armor Girl, so get over yourself.

Number 3: Heath is still not as hot as the hottie Schwerinborg prince Christie and Natalie and I read about on the Internet. The one the article said lives in the same palace you do. The one named Georg. (Did his parents forget the "e" in George? Or is that some bizarro Schwerinborg thing?!)

Number 4: You have still not written me back to say what happened when you gave Hottie Prince Georg, mentioned in item Number 3, my phone number and e-mail address.

Number 5: If you haven't done it yet, I'm going to kick your ass. You're on a tight time line here, Val, because we KNOW you're coming home soon. RIGHT? So go accidentally and on purpose bump into my future boyfriend and GIVE HIM

MY E-MAIL!! I am not joking about the ass-kicking and you know it.

The future princess of Smorgasbord, Jules

TWO

I suppose if I get married to Georg some-day, I might actually be a princess. Someday being very, very far away, and not even remotely on my brain, especially given the wonderful example of wedded bliss I've witnessed with my parents recently.

But no matter what Christie says, I am definitely not *David's* princess, at least not like Shallow Princess was for Heath in *A Knight's Tale*. Not even close.

I switch off my computer without answering Christie's e-mail. I know she means well, but I just can't deal right now. I'll think of something brilliant to say while I'm at school—something that'll get her off my case about David but that won't hurt her feelings. Since we're six hours ahead of Virginia, I'll be home long before Christie gets to check her in-box, so she'll assume I answered right away and won't be offended.

And Jules's e-mail just needs to be ignored. For now, at least. Despite her ass-kicking threats, I know she's kidding. Well, I hope.

Geez, I wish they hadn't all popped "Schwerinborg" into Google when I moved here. Or at least that they hadn't found out all about the royal family, and about Georg.

I toss my backpack over my shoulder, give the apartment one last look to make sure I haven't forgotten anything I need for school, then lock the door behind me, since of course Dad was up bright and early this morning to go work for Prince Manfred. He's very efficient—he wakes up at five A.M. most mornings so he can go to the gym. (Yes, my dad is a hottie, as far as dads go, and no, I try not to think about the way women are constantly scoping out his bod, because the whole idea of some

Schwerinborg woman doing my dad is beyond revolting.) Then he takes a shower and gets dressed in one of his expensive suits (always gray, black, or navy blue) and is out the door by six thirty.

Usually, it annoys me that he's so perfectly scheduled, but it worked in my favor last night. He went straight to bed when he got home, so he didn't even realize Georg was in my room when he came in.

I still can't believe Georg and I weren't more careful about watching the clock.

Okay, maybe I can believe it. Georg has this way of making me feel so incredible when we're together—and not just when we're making out—that I have trouble keeping focused on anything else going on around me. This is totally corny, but he makes me feel better about *me*.

As I walk down the palace halls zipping my coat, I realize I've got to tell the girls in Virginia about Georg. Somehow. They're going to be all excited by the fact I'm with a prince, but I just know they'll be royally (pardon the pun) pissed off at the same time, partially because of the David Anderson thing, and partially because they're girly-girls and they won't like that I didn't tell them about Georg the very instant I met him—because who meets a prince every day?—let alone that I waited to tell them we're an actual couple.

And even though they won't say it, probably even to each other, they're also going to think it's not fair that I get to live in a palace and date a prince, especially when all three of them are better looking than me. Well, Christie is definitely better looking—she's tall and blonde and has a gorgeous, zit-free face, not to mention boobage. The kind most women get implanted. Jules and Natalie are fairly good-looking, too—they're your typical cute brunettes. And Jules has the kind of attitude you'd think a world-wise prince would go for. (Which is probably why she had no qualms about ordering me to give Georg her e-mail addy and phone number.)

But me, I'm a red-haired freak of nature. I'm so pale I practically glow in the dark, and I'm pretty ordinary personality-wise. Not great, not bad, just perfectly *average*.

But the thing is—and this is the

primary reason I haven't had the guts to tell my friends about Georg—they won't get it. They'll be all starry-eyed, equating Georg with the celebs we drool over during awards shows. They won't realize that Georg is a *real person,* and that Georg and I have conversations about normal stuff like the whacked things our parents and our teachers do, and what kinds of music we like, and how soccer's going for him. They'll think—which, admittedly, I did at first—that his life is full of parties and that he can do whatever he wants, whenever he wants, because he's famous (well, in Europe, anyway) and he has tons of money.

They'll wonder what the hell he's doing with me, and conclude that I'm just some temporary Armor Girl holding his hand until a mega-wealthy, Prada-wearing, Euro-society girl comes along to hold it. It's also occurred to me that they might think I'm lying, either because I'm lonely over here in Schwerinborg and want attention, or to make them stop pestering me about David.

I guess I can't blame them, though. I pestered *them* about David for years. Like, ever since David and I were assigned to take care of the class rabbit together in kindergarten and I fell hard for the guy and his way-blue eyes and slightly off-kilter smile. Someone who's lusted after a guy the way I've lusted after David doesn't just turn around one day and announce they're seeing someone else—especially when the target of their lust is finally interested. *If* he's really interested.

"Hey, Valerie." Georg's smooth voice makes me jump as I reach for the handle on the door that leads outside, the one I use when I'm walking to school because it's at the back of the palace and cuts five minutes off my walk.

I turn to see Georg leaning against the wall, waiting for me and looking absolutely yummy in his black leather coat, a dark green sweater, and a pair of Levi's. A sudden sour taste—guilt?—rises in my mouth at the sound of his voice, and I mentally chew myself out for even thinking of David.

"Hey back," I say. "Please tell me you didn't get caught sneaking back into your room last night. I was really worried."

He gives me a *who me?* look. "My parents were already in their room, getting ready for bed, talking about some meeting my father's having with the Greek ambassador tomorrow, when I got back. I think they assumed I was already asleep. My door was shut exactly the way I'd left it. I got past without them noticing."

"What about the security guys?" There are two very burly men with guns who stand outside the doors to the part of the palace where Georg and his parents live.

He shrugs. "They're supposed to keep stuff private. And they didn't know I wasn't allowed out, anyway."

I shake my head at him. "Lucky for you."

"Very lucky." He shoots me a grin that's downright sinful, then makes a show of looking past me to see if we're alone in the hall. He pulls me off to the side, behind this big pedestal with a statue of one of his long-dead ancestors on top of it, and gives me a devastating kiss.

A few minutes later, he eases back and whispers, "I missed you, Val."

"It's only been about six hours."

"I know." He leans forward so his forehead's against mine and gives me a slow, incredibly sexy smile, one he knows is going to make me melt inside. "But I missed you anyway."

I shift my gaze toward the door. Since we both have to be at school in twenty minutes, and it's a fifteen-minute walk, we'd better get going. "You want to go first, or should I?"

"Let's walk together."

"I thought we were going to keep this quiet?" Given how close a call we had last night, I'm thinking we should be extra careful today. Last time the reporter was around, Georg walked way ahead of me on the way to school—and nothing had even happened between us then.

"Well, I wasn't planning to hold your hand or make out with you in the middle of the street," he teases, playing with the shoulder strap of my backpack. "We shouldn't be suspicious if we just walk together like normal friends."

I go to the door and take a peek out. I even stick my hand outside, like I'm trying to determine whether it's raining or just misty, while I'm subtly taking a look around.

"I haven't seen him," Georg says from behind me. "He doesn't usually do Mondays. Tuesdays and Fridays seem to be the days, though he does mix it up sometimes."

I ease the door most of the way shut. "I didn't see him, either, but—"

"Then let's go." He reaches past me and opens the door, then holds it so I can go first.

I can't resist him when he's being chivalrous.

When we're about halfway to school, Georg fishes a few euros out of his pocket and walks up to a coffee stand. The people who live and work along this street are used to seeing Georg every day, so the guy selling coffee and muffins doesn't freak out or anything. He just says hello—well, he actually says, *"Guten Morgen,"* which is German for "good morning"—and hands out a tall latte, Georg's favorite, while I stand a little farther back on the cobblestoned street and rub my shoe over one of the gray stones, wondering how my life could have changed so much in just a few weeks.

When I look up, the coffee guy smiles at me and asks what I want. At least, I think that's what he's asking. I'm about to say, *"Nichts, danke"*—"nothing, thanks"—it being about the extent of my German, not because I don't want any coffee, but because I spaced asking Dad for more cash this morning. But Georg goes right ahead and orders me a cappuccino, just the way I like it, with nonfat milk and cinnamon. He talks a little bit with the coffee guy, and though I can't understand a word of it, I can tell they're pretty friendly with each other.

"You're such a prince," I tease him once we get away from the stand, each of us warming our hands with our paper to-go cups.

"I've heard that before," he says. He's grinning sideways at me, and it's so magical, I try to capture the moment in my head so I can sketch it later. I love to sketch people, and the way he's looking at me now would be so great to draw. There's so much texture—his scarf, wrapped perfectly around his neck and disappearing into the V where his leather jacket is zipped up; the way his long fingers are wrapped around the coffee as the steam curls up out of the tiny hole in the lid; and, best of all, when he looks at me with his head tilted to the side, his cheekbones look freaking fantastic. He's regal and normal at the same time.

"You're making a mental drawing, aren't you?" he asks after he takes another sip of his latte.

I'm about to make a sarcastic reply when he stops short. I follow his gaze down the sidewalk in the direction we're headed, and realize the *Majesty* magazine guy is standing right in front of us. His blond hair is messed up from the wind, but he's completely ignoring it because he has out a camera with a monster lens and is snapping away.

Georg puts his head down and starts walking again, so I do the same. But all of a sudden, I'm feeling like I have rocks in my stomach and I can't drink my cappuccino.

"He doesn't usually take pictures, does he?" I ask as quietly as possible, since the guy's only about twenty feet in front of us and walking backward.

"Not very often. He must have space to fill in the paper. Just pretend he's not there." He says this in a whisper, so it's hard for me to tell if he's bothered by this too. I'm guessing we won't walk to school together tomorrow.

We turn the corner onto the street leading to our school. It's an American high school—all the teachers are Americans—and most of the kids have parents who work for the government or are in the country temporarily for one reason or another. Ulrike's dad's a German diplomat, for instance. Maya is from New York. Her family moved over here when her mother got a job with some big investment bank. There are a few kids who've always lived here, like Georg, but they go to school here because all the classes are taught in English, and their parents want them to be fluent.

Thankfully, because it's a private school, the reporter apparently has to stay a certain number of feet back, off school property. Just before we go past the school gate, though, he asks, "Prince Georg, would you care to talk about your relationship with Miss Winslow?"

"Miss Winslow's father works at the palace," Georg says, sounding totally casual. But I'm so shocked, I stop cold. This guy knows *my name*?

"Valerie, you'd better hurry or you're going to be late." Georg says this to me from just inside the gate. He doesn't look alarmed or anything, but I can tell from his tone that he wants me to ignore the guy and get inside the gate, pronto.

I hike my backpack further up on my shoulder and walk in, leaving the reporter out on the cobblestoned street. Once we're out of earshot, Georg says, "He's never spoken to me before, which means he thinks he knows something. Someone's tipped him off."

"He knew my name." How is this possible? I mean, Georg and I had our first real date on *Friday*. And even then, no one but my dad and Georg's parents knew it was an actual date. Georg's parents promised to tell any reporters who asked that we weren't "romantically involved," but that they'd invited me to the reception because my father was working there, and so Georg would have another teenager to talk to during the event.

We reach the door that leads to where all the sophomore lockers—excuse me, *year ten* lockers—are located on the first floor. Since Georg is in year eleven, he has to take the staircase just inside the door to the second floor, where he has his locker. But instead of going into the building and then us going our separate ways like I expected, he grabs my elbow and steers me a few steps away from the door, so we can talk in private.

"Georg, how could that guy possibly know my name? I'm a *nobody*."

"You're not a nobody—"

"You know what I mean."

"I know what you mean," Georg says with a drawn-out sigh. He takes a long sip of his latte, looking over the lid to make sure no one's watching us too closely. "I've walked to school with friends before—I do it all the time—and he's never once bothered them or taken their picture. Well, he's taken *mine,* but not theirs."

I'm starting to really freak out now, but Georg says very calmly, "I think he's just fishing, Valerie. That's why he asked his question in English instead of German—so you would understand. He was probably hoping you'd make a comment."

"That still doesn't explain how he knew my name. At the reception on Friday, no one asked who I was. Your parents didn't tell anyone. So . . ." I hold my hands out and give him a *what the hell is going on?* stare.

Georg frowns, and it's clear he has no answer, so I ask the more important question. "What are we going to do now?"

"Nothing," he says, keeping his voice low as a group of guys walk by, give us a quick look, then go through the door on their way to class. "Just act normal and pretend it didn't happen. And if you see the reporter on your way home, ignore him. In the meantime, I'll call my father on my cell and let him know about it."

"He's going to be ticked off."

Georg runs his hand over his dark hair, something he does only when he's exasperated, even though he's sounding completely

Zen. "He'll be unhappy with the reporter, not with us. And if I let him know about it, he can tell us how to handle it."

"Okay." I take a deep breath just as the warning bell rings. "We'd better hurry. I'll see you tonight?"

He gives me the kind of smile you give someone when you want them to feel better. "Definitely."

But as I scoot into French IV, I realize I don't feel better at all.

By lunch, I feel like I'm ready to hurl.

I grab a very normal-looking turkey sandwich from the cafeteria (usually they have bulkie rolls with unidentifiable contents—stuff I've taken to calling Unknown Meat of Germanic Origin) and head out to the quad. I want to find Georg. I want to hear what Prince Manfred said about the whole reporter thing. I want to hear that this is just me and my wacky imagination, and that no one knows anything and even if they did, it's no big thing.

What I get is Ulrike, Maya, and Steffi—which would be fine except for

Steffi, who's looking at me like I stole my turkey sandwich out of her backpack or something.

"Hey, Valerie!" Ulrike waves me over to their picnic table—there are a few dozen of them around the quad—and offers me the seat next to her. While I unwrap the sandwich and pop the top on a Coke Light (since, here in Schwerinborg, it's *Coke Light,* not Diet Coke), they all yak and yak about what happened in their classes during the morning, and who saw what movies and who went where over the weekend.

I'm scanning the quad for Georg, and I must be obvious, because of course Steffi asks me about it. I can tell from her face she'd been talking to Ulrike and Maya about Georg before I sat down. Heinous-evil-bitch-girl.

"Yeah, he wanted to talk to me about something," I say, trying to sound as casual as possible while I fumble to make something up. "Probably some palace security thing. Who knows?"

I see Maya shoot Ulrike a look. I want to yell, *What?* but think better of it. Then

Steffi gives Ulrike this exaggerated look of concern that's so fake, I want to smack her.

"Valerie, did you see Georg this weekend?" Ulrike turns to me and asks.

"Well, since we live in the same building, yeah," I say. I don't say it in a snotty way at all—more like, *sure, hard not to see him*. But since I'm guessing they already know about the dinner, I add, "And he was at this formal thing of Prince Manfred's Friday night that my father brought me to. I think my dad wanted me to keep Georg company, since he was the only other person there under the age of forty."

Maya's eyes get wide, but she looks down at her Tupperware container and takes a bite of salad.

Now I'm so sick to my stomach I can't even choke down my turkey, so I take a long sip of my soda. Why, why, why, WHY did I come out to the quad, when I should have known something like this would happen? And where the hell is Georg?!

Ulrike sets down her sandwich. "Valerie, I hope you don't take offense, but"—she looks at Steffi, as if she needs to know it's okay to tell me something awful—"but at the reception, did you offer Georg drugs?"

I laugh out loud at this. I mean, I know it's not a laughing matter, but are they freaking kidding me?

"Someone told you I gave Georg *drugs*?" Then I realize that they're dead serious. "That's insane! I've never even smoked pot or anything, ever."

Geez, I knew there were probably going to be rumors about me and Georg, but at least this one I know I can argue. I look Ulrike—then Steffi—square in the eye and say, "Whoever told you guys that story is the one on drugs."

They all look totally shocked, which makes me wonder who I could possibly have offended when *I'm* the one who should be totally offended.

Geez. Even if I was a total cokehead or pothead or whatever, I'm not stupid enough to give drugs to a FREAKING PRINCE!

Then Steffi gives me this sad, sympathetic look that I know is for the sole purpose of making Ulrike and Maya think she's all choked up about the situation. "It was the minister of the treasury. He saw you and Georg on Friday night, and he says you were trying to give Prince Georg drugs."

The minister of the treasury?! He's the guy who was so smashed at the dinner that my dad had to help him into the bathroom before he puked in public—like, all over Princess Claudia's shoes. I didn't think the guy even saw me and Georg, he was so plowed, but apparently he did.

And completely mistook what he saw for something else.

"Well, he's way wrong," I say. "You can ask Georg."

"No, we can't," Maya finally speaks up. "He went home about an hour ago. Someone from the palace came in a big limo and picked him up."

"Then ask him tomorrow. Or call him on his cell," I tell them. Now I'm getting angry, because I know the truth. And I know Steffi's going to spread this rumor fast and furious if I give her the chance, because she'd do anything to make certain I don't get together with Georg. "You guys might not believe me—even though you *should*—but you've known Georg forever, and you know he wouldn't lie to you about something like this."

"Please don't think we're mad at you, or that we're accusing you of anything, Valerie," Ulrike says. "I mean, there are tons of people here who are into stuff they shouldn't be. But——"

"Look, I know you're a really nice person, and that you're not trying to hurt my feelings." I say this to Ulrike, though I'd say the same thing to Maya, too, if it wouldn't make it obvious that I think Steffi's an incredible bitch by leaving her out "——but I would never give anyone drugs, let alone do them myself. The worst I've ever done in my life is smoke a cigarette, and it's been ages since I've done that. Seriously."

Well, since I was in Virginia, at least. And even then, it wasn't a regular thing at all. "And all of you had better talk to Georg before you spread any rumors"——this time I look directly at Steffi, because I'm deciding I have nothing to lose, and no way am I going to take her shit——"or you're really going to hurt his reputation and his family."

47

I wrap my sandwich back up in its plastic wrap, because there's no way I'm going to eat it now. It'd come right back up. It'd be about as ugly as the treasury guy was, hurling all over one of the men's room stalls on Friday night while my dad tried to clean him up and shuffle me and Georg out of the handicapped stall at the same time.

I stand up to leave, but a thought occurs to me and I turn to Ulrike. "Hey, your dad was at that dinner Friday night. He saw me there, and Georg, too. He'll tell you we weren't doing anything like that."

She blushes all the way from the neck of her peach sweater to the roots of her white-blond hair, and I realize she's the source of the rumor. The treasury minister must've told her father, and he told her.

And Ulrike, of course, told Steffi, thinking she was being helpful or something. Because as nice as Ulrike is, she's too naive to see through Steffi.

"Well, he's wrong," I say. I can feel my throat getting tight, so I force myself to keep my voice steady and calm, the way Georg would. "Way wrong. Call Georg. He'll tell you the truth, even if you don't believe me."

Three

"Valerie? Can you come out here?"

I roll my eyes but yell out in a friendly voice, "Just a sec, Dad!"

When Dad calls for me instead of knocking on my door, it usually means he has something serious to discuss. And I have one guess what it is this time.

Geez, but I wish Georg would call me. I sent him an e-mail and left a message on his cell the second I got home from school, but nada. Nothing. Zip.

I'm guessing he ended up going back to school for soccer practice, in which case he can't call me back, but I have no way of knowing for sure. And how the hell am I going to handle my dad if I don't know what's going on with Georg?

I shove my Geometry book off my lap, stick my pencil and calculator in the page—not that I've been able to focus on it, since I've been replaying my lunchtime conversation over and over in my head, wondering what I should have said—then climb off my bed and go out to the living room.

Dad's standing in our galley kitchen, putting chicken breasts in a pan for dinner. He's humming to himself and smiling, but since he hardly even got mad at my mother when she made her little "It's not you, it's me" divorce announcement out of the blue, the fact he's not growling or anything doesn't give me much hope.

"You need me to chop veggies?" I ask, deciding to play innocent for as long as possible.

"Nope, I'll do it while the chicken bakes. I just wanted to make sure we have a few minutes to talk." He takes a bowl full of some yellowish marinade he's whipped up and pours it over the raw chicken. As disgusting as that sounds, it looks and smells completely delish, and my stomach starts this loud, low rumble. Partially because I know my dad is incapable of making bad food, and partially because, due to circumstances beyond my control, I didn't eat lunch.

As Dad slides the pan into the oven, he asks, just a little too casually, "So school was all right today?"

"Same teachers, same homework."

"And things are going well with Georg, honey?"

Oh, crap. "Sure."

I just know I'm going to hate this conversation. I bet he knows Georg was here last night. He's smart about stuff like that. And that's just going to make him even more ticked off, especially if he already knows about everything that went down at school today.

But I'm still going to eat that chicken and enjoy it.

"I talked to Prince Manfred this afternoon. I understand a reporter followed you two to school this morning?"

I open a cupboard and snag a cookie, even though I know this is tempting fate.

Dad hates when I get snacky before dinner. "Yeah. He writes articles about Georg every so often. I think that happens when you're royalty."

He pins me with a stare that I know has nothing to do with the cookie. "But today the reporter asked Georg about his relationship with you. Right?"

I give him my I-don't-care shrug. Dad calls it the Valerie Shrug, which is his way of telling he can see right through me, but I do it anyway. "Georg just told him you work at the palace. After that, the reporter left us alone."

Dad raises an eyebrow.

"Okay, we were at the gate to school, so he kind of had to leave us alone. But it's not a big deal." I don't think.

"Unfortunately, it is a big deal, Valerie. The reporter called the protocol office today and said he wanted to ask me a few questions. I didn't return his call, but I'll have to tomorrow."

Dad takes off his apron and loops it over a hook inside our tiny pantry. I know, it's weird he wears an apron, but he claims all good cooks wear aprons to protect their clothing. Since he feeds me all his wonderful creations, I never say a word about the apron.

I mean, I have serious food issues. Not starvation or dieting issues, or how-fat-do-I-look-in-this-outfit? issues, but you-can-get-me-to-say-or-do-anything-if-you-feed-me-well issues. Dad knows this and uses it to his advantage all the time. It is not a coincidence that he called me out of my room to talk while making dinner. He wants me to smell the chicken.

"So what are you going to tell him?"

"Nothing—not unless Prince Manfred wants to issue a statement. But I wanted to warn you. You're always careful, honey, but it may not be enough to simply be careful."

I polish off the cookie and ask, "Should I not walk to school with Georg?"

"Maybe not every day." He takes a deep breath, then crosses his arms over his chest. "I know you two have just started seeing each other, but dating Georg isn't going to be like dating anyone else, Valerie, and I want you to understand the gravity of that. The media feel they have a right to poke into your life if you're associated with someone who's in the news."

"Like with you, when you were at the White House?"

"Exactly."

The whole media thing is the reason Dad had to move to Schwerinborg. It's an election year, and President Carew is a very conservative Republican. Not only is he pro-gun, pro-life, and pro–big business, he's completely anti–gay rights. And in an election year, you don't want your protocol chief's wife suddenly coming out of the closet. Stuff like that tends to turn up on Fox News, when someone like Bill O'Reilly asks the president how he can be anti–gay rights when one of his employees is married to a lesbian, especially if he's had that employee and his family to dinner at the White House numerous times and they're "personal friends." (We're definitely not personal friends, but Dad says that's how the question would get asked on the Sunday morning political shows.)

So President Carew, out of the goodness of his heart (I think he has a heart, maybe), found Dad this job in Schwerinborg and promised to bring him back to the White House after the election. Dad's worked for three U.S. presidents, so he's the best there is. Even if Carew loses the election, the new president is bound to try to hire my dad back. But still. I know it's tough on Dad not being at the White House, even if he likes working for Prince Manfred and Princess Claudia.

"Well, maybe not exactly like the White House," he corrects himself. He gets a slightly sad look on his face, and I feel guilty for bringing it up. "There, I brought my situation upon myself to a certain extent. I knew when I took the job that I had to"—he hesitates for a second, because he's always careful about how he phrases things—"I had to sanitize my life, in many ways. But I never expected you to have to be so careful, which is why we lived in Vienna, and why I didn't take you to the White House or to government events very often."

"To protect me?"

"Yes." He smiles at me in a way that lets me know he really loves me and views me as an adult—that he's not just saying all this to exert his Dad Authority over me. "Reporters can be very, very nasty about personal issues, whether you're fifteen or fifty. If they suspect you and Georg are dating, they're going to dig into your personal life, and they won't be kinder in their approach just because you're not yet an adult."

"My personal life is boring. I mean, I get straight A's, and it's not like they're going to dig up some hacked-off ex-boyfriend to talk trash about me." Because I don't have any.

"But you were in trouble last year in Vienna when you were caught smoking behind the school." He pauses for a second, and looks me in the eye. This time, he definitely has the Dad Authority look. "And apparently the minister of the treasury saw you in the bathroom stall with Georg. He's mentioned it to at least one other person."

Yeah, no kidding.

So I ask Dad the question that's been bugging me all afternoon. "Why would he do that? I mean, the guy was puking his guts out. You wouldn't think he'd want anyone to know."

My dad lets out a totally uncharacteristic grunt. "That's exactly why he did it. To cover himself. A number of people saw him drinking at the event—drinking heavily—and they know he disappeared for a while. I'd be stunned if a reporter or two didn't notice. But when a friend asked if he was all right, rather than making an excuse or dodging the question, the treasury minister claimed to have been in the restroom longer than usual because he saw something disturbing."

"Me and Georg." And I can guess which friend asked him if he was all right: Ulrike's dad. The guy's probably just as well-meaning and just as naive about people's motives as Ulrike, though you'd think a diplomat—even someone assigned to boring Schwerinborg—would be a little more attuned to people's bullshit.

"Yes. The minister told your friend Ulrike's father that he saw you and Georg huddled in a bathroom stall, and that he feared you were hiding in there to do drugs. He claimed he stayed in the restroom for several minutes to make sure you two weren't doing anything illicit."

I close my eyes for a sec to absorb this. I had no idea things could be this bad. So much for this being solely Steffi's fault.

"Of course," Dad says, "Ulrike's father knew the whole idea was ridiculous, and told the treasury minister he knew better—he watched me escort the minister out of the room when the minister was feeling ill. Ulrike's father went to Prince Manfred right away—not to get either of you in trouble, but to ensure that any rumors would be stopped immediately. He knew the treasury minister was intoxicated, and he was worried that the minister might have told the same story to others."

"So Ulrike's dad was trying to protect you or something?"

"He was trying to protect all of us—Georg's family and the two of us. Prince Manfred spoke to the treasury minister this morning. The minister apologized and admitted that he behaved badly at the party—both by becoming intoxicated, then by using you and Georg as an excuse to cover his own inappropriate behavior. So the issue has been handled."

I'm thinking, not quite, since Ulrike's dad clearly told her, and she told Steffi, who has the biggest mouth in the universe. "So no harm, no foul?"

"That's what we thought, until Georg told his father about the reporter following you two to school today. Prince Manfred is worried that something may have leaked. It's too much of a coincidence. Both the minister and Ulrike's father insist they haven't said a word to anyone else, and would never corroborate a news story about it since they know it's not true, but you never know what someone might've overheard, or what that person might be saying to others."

Yeah, like Ulrike overhearing and telling Steffi, thinking she was being helpful by preventing me from trying to get Georg hooked on drugs or something.

I've got to tell Ulrike this was all a mistake. She'll understand. I can't say anything to Steffi, but maybe if Ulrike hears the real story, Steffi will get a clue too.

As I brush the crumbs from my cookie into the trash, my eye catches a book on the table out in the living room. Mom sent it to me—she has this thing about self-help books—and all of a sudden, I have a duh moment.

I turn back around to look at Dad. "You know I'm clean, right? I study and don't cut school, and that the smoking thing is totally over, and I've never touched drugs of any kind?"

One side of his mouth curves up. "Yes, I know. You work hard, and I'm proud of you."

"Then what are you really afraid of the tabloids finding out? Are you afraid that a reporter might write about you and Mom?"

He gives me one of his *you're smarter than you should be* looks. "It has occurred to me. Europeans are far more accepting of homosexuality than most Americans, but it still makes good tabloid copy. They'll find a way to twist what happened with me and your mother to question Georg's choices, or to question the manner in which Prince Manfred and Princess Claudia are raising Georg."

"That's insane."

"It's reality. Tabloids will print whatever they can in order to sell more papers, and hope that it's close enough to the truth to keep them from getting sued."

I grab two green peppers out of the

fridge since I know he's going to chop them and add them to the chicken when it's done, and I carry them to the sink. I have a sick feeling about what Dad's going to say next and I don't want to get all teary. I'm not the wussy crybaby type at all, but I need to not look at him for a sec.

As I turn on the faucet to wash the peppers, I ask, "Does Prince Manfred think it'd be better if I stayed away from Georg?"

"No, but he is concerned about both of you." My dad takes the peppers out of my hands and puts them on the counter. "I didn't tell him about the cigarette incident. However, if the press sees you smoking around Georg, or if he is caught smoking—"

"I told you, we *weren't* smoking. Those were in there when we got there." It's the truth. We weren't, and they were there when we got there.

"You're missing my point, honey. Do you think a reporter would care if the cigarettes were already there? If a reporter sees you smoking, or even with a pack in your hand, he's going to snap a photo. Europeans smoke more than Americans, but they still don't want their princes doing it. Plus, a reporter could use that photo to hint that you and Georg are doing other things you shouldn't be doing, and that'll open all this up again."

I force myself to look at him. I'm completely surprised to see he's not angry with me, just overly worried. "I'll be careful, Dad. Please believe that I'm not smoking, and that I won't."

"I believe you." I see a little muscle twitch in his cheek, so I know he's making an effort not to get worked up about this. "Maybe it was wrong to use cigarettes as an example. It could be anything you do. Anything that can be twisted to show that you don't appreciate European culture. Speeding. Littering. Treating service providers like waiters or desk clerks badly. Do you understand?"

I nod. If I didn't get it before, I sure do now.

"And I think Georg is terrific. If you recall, I'm the one who took you dress and shoe shopping before your big night out."

"True." And he did a fabulous job, too—when the shoe clerks weren't flirting with him. Of course, the way he's looking at me now, I know there's a big but coming.

"But," he says, true to form, "I think you and Georg need to have a long talk about this before you take your relationship much further. All right? Georg isn't going to be like any other boyfriend."

Like I've had any other boyfriend to compare him to. "I'm not sure what there is to talk about, though. We won't do anything stupid, especially in public."

"If you need advice, I know a very good protocol expert." He smiles, but I know he's dead serious. "If anything, anything at all, feels off to you, like that encounter with the reporter this morning, I want you to tell me immediately."

The buzzer on the stove goes off, and Dad grabs his cup of marinade so he can pour the rest of it over the chicken since it's midway through cooking. I'm tempted to tell him about what happened with Steffi—since apparently he doesn't know that the treasury minister and Ulrike's dad were definitely overheard, probably on the phone after the party—but I figure it's probably nothing. Just Steffi being her usual bitchy self. Once I talk to Ulrike, things will be cool on that front. And who knows? Maybe her father's already talked to her if he thinks she overheard, and I'll show up at school tomorrow and everyone will apologize.

It's a long shot, but I'm willing to pin my hopes on it.

Dad glances over his shoulder at me as he closes the door to the stove. "Are we understood?"

"As long as you give me the big piece of chicken."

Because what I really understand is that if things don't go well tomorrow, then I'll tell him.

To: Val@realmail.sg.com
From: BarbnGabby@mailmagic.com
Subject: RE: Everything

Dear Valerie,

I hope you and your father are enjoying life in Schwerinborg. As you can imagine, I'm envious of all the rich culture and fine cuisine you must be enjoying there!

Speaking of European food, how did your fancy dinner date go on Friday night? I wish I'd been there to see you in your new dress. Your father said you looked like a movie star. (Of course, I've always thought that.) I'm so excited for you, sweetheart.

You might want to check your mail over the next few days—I know you said not to send any more books, but I saw one I just couldn't resist, and I think it'll help you keep your head on straight where boys are concerned. Not that I'm worried about Prince Georg—I'm sure he's quite the gentleman—but indulge me. I can't turn off the Mom urge simply because you're far away.

I'm still waiting to hear on the teaching job. I'll keep you posted. And you know, if you decide you'd like to come back and visit during Winter Break, you're more than welcome. Gabrielle would love to get to know you better, and I simply miss you.

Lots of love,
Mom

The second sentence of Mom's morning e-mail makes me laugh aloud, because ever since she moved in with Gabrielle she's been living on things like wheatgrass and quinoa. If I were in her place, I'd be envious of my food, too, even if it is wacky Euro-McDonald's half the time as I'm walking home from school. (And really, if she places such a high priority on good food, she should have stayed married to Dad.)

But the rest bugs me. Does Mom really think I need all the self-help books? I mean, she's always had an addiction to them, and I did say nice things to her after she sent me the first one . . . but I also specifically stated that she should not send another.

I so do not want to live life according to the publicity junkie, pseudo relationship expert of the moment. Especially my love life. I mean, if Dr. Phil knows so much about dating celebrities, why is he hawking books on *Oprah* while wearing a bad suit instead of living in a mansion with some Pam Anderson wanna-be and attending pool parties?

And I won't even start on the teaching thing. Mom taught school before I was born and swore she'd never do it again. I mean, I know Dad is giving her whatever she wants in the divorce—he's practically paying for her and Gabrielle's apartment himself. (It's really disgusting and pathetic, if you think about it.) So I don't get why she's in such a rush to get back to work, when she could take her time, think about something else she might want to do, and then go do that.

I click on the Reply button to: 1) tell her there's now an official moratorium on self-help books, because even if I wanted them, I have no time to read them and no space to store them in my itty bitty bedroom; and 2) she should really think about it before she starts teaching school again. Because as ticked off as I am about her and Gabrielle and the whole divorce (I try not to be, but I can't help it), I don't want her to be miserable.

Just as I start to type, the phone rings and I grab it. The only people who'd call me before school are my mom—which saves me typing time—or Georg. And I really, really want to talk to him so he knows what's up.

But it's Ulrike. And I think she's crying.

"Valerie? I just wanted to say I'm so sorry. I hope you're not too mad. I swear it wasn't me, but I might have been the cause of—"

"Of what?" She sure didn't seem this worked up yesterday at lunch. I'm wondering if she got in some major trouble. Or if she called Georg like I asked her to do and he read her the riot act.

Not that Georg would read anyone the riot act. He doesn't get visibly angry about anything. He's totally cool that way.

"Well, you should be mad, but I'm—"

"Ulrike, seriously, I'm not mad at you."

At exactly that moment, Dad knocks on my bedroom door, scaring me half out of the chair. It's nearly seven thirty, so the man should be at work. I cover the phone and yell that I'll be just a sec.

"Ulrike, I've gotta go. My dad's knocking on my door."

"But—"

"Hey, we'll talk at school. I'll try to get

there early and meet you in the year ten hallway, okay? But it's no big deal, really. I know you were just trying to protect Georg."

"Okay. But I'm so sorry, Valerie."

I roll my eyes as I hang up. Ulrike's too nice for her own good.

My dad knocks again, louder this time, and I'm about to say something I probably shouldn't, like *what the hell?*, when he walks in.

He holds up the newspaper. Not just one of the ratty tabloids, but a regular, honest-to-goodness newspaper. And there I am on the front page. In color.

You'd think the picture would catch my attention, since it's of me and Georg on our walk to school yesterday. Not because it's a good picture—both of us have our backpacks over our shoulders, and my hair is flying all over the place and I look highly annoyed—and not that I didn't kind of expect to see something about us in the paper. It's more the angle. The photo is taken from the side, so it couldn't have been the *Majesty* reporter. In fact, I'm certain I look annoyed in the photo because if it was much bigger, the *Majesty* reporter would be in it, since it looks like it was taken at the exact moment the guy asked Georg about his relationship with me.

But no. I don't give a fly about the picture, or the fact that the *Majesty* guy obviously wasn't the only shutterbug around. And I'm guessing Dad isn't concerned about the photo, either.

It's the screaming headline.

Four

"Oh, shit!"

As soon as the words are out, I slam a hand over my mouth, because I can't believe I said what I just said in front of Dad. I mean, as if I haven't screwed myself enough here with the headline alone.

I don't have to know German to translate the two-inch-high type. It says something to the effect of:

THE BAD AMERICAN . . . ?

I think it means bad. Maybe evil or dangerous. Whatever it is, it's definitely not good, even if they did pose the headline in the form of a question, *Jeopardy!* style.

I look at my dad to gauge his reaction,

and I realize things must be really bad, because he isn't even pissed at me for swearing, despite the fact I have never, ever said anything like that around him before.

Normally, I'm pretty sure he'd kill me. Martin Winslow is all about polite and proper behavior, and swearing is at the top of his Not To Do list. But instead of jumping all over me, giving me a lecture about how a young lady doesn't use words like that, he just shoots me a *you can say that again* grimace that makes me think he's already uttered a few four-letter words himself.

"Who was on the phone?" he asks, nodding toward the receiver.

"Ulrike."

His eyebrows jerk up. "Was she calling about the article?"

"We just started talking when you knocked, so I don't know." Her tearful I'm sorry's make more sense, though, if she was. "Maybe."

Oh, crap. Not only does the headline mean everyone will know about it—it means half the school already knows about it. They're probably IM'ing one another right now, yakking about the whole thing, debating whether THE BAD AMERICAN is really bad or evil or whatever.

I bet Steffi's borderline orgasmic.

Dad takes a deep breath, the kind adults make when they're really worked up about something and are trying to stay calm, where you can actually hear the air whooshing in and out of their nostrils.

"All right. No more telephone for the time being—not unless I hand you the receiver. Let me answer if it rings."

"I was about to leave for school, anyway." I have to be there in about half an hour, so it's not like I'm going to be calling everyone and asking if they saw the gigantic headline.

"Let's hold off for a while. If you go, I'll drive you there. Definitely no walking today."

Wow. I've never been allowed to skip school. I hate to ask, but I do anyway. "So what does the article say, exactly?"

"I assume you can figure out the headline?"

"I think so. Enough to know it's not good."

Dad pushes my door the rest of the way open and hands me the newspaper, then walks over to my bed and sits down while I stare at the front page.

"Prince Manfred says it essentially means 'The Corrupt American.' Of course, they added an ellipse and question mark after it, as if to suggest your level of corruption is open to debate, but I don't think that makes it much better."

I'm thinking not, either. "Well, no matter what the article itself says, I'm not corrupt. I mean, *corrupt* makes it sound like I'm embezzling money from the royal family or something."

Not that I'd have the foggiest clue how to do that. I'm not even sure what embezzle means, exactly, other than something to do with stealing. Guess I'd better find out before the SATs. Now that I think about it, *embezzle* strikes me as an SAT word.

Dad shifts on the bed, and it's clear this whole conversation is giving him a headache. "The article states that there are unsubstantiated—and Prince Manfred said it uses that word, *unsubstantiated*, several times—rumors that you and Georg are close. It doesn't come out and say you're dating, but it strongly hints at it. It also states that you left the Friday night reception together, then were seen entering an unused restroom on a lower floor of the palace."

"Oh." I don't know what else to say. I'm just staring at the words on the page, wishing they were in English. Or even French, since my French is pretty good. I want to read this for myself, and it's killing me that it's just a bunch of funny-looking words I can hardly pronounce, let alone understand.

"So, where does the corrupt part come in?" I can hear the *Jeopardy!* music playing in my head as I stare at Dad, because I just know it's gonna be the whole druggie thing Ulrike talked about.

"The article doesn't hint that you and Georg could have been going into that restroom to take drugs. Again, it doesn't make a definitive claim, but anyone reading the article can draw that conclusion."

And there the *Jeopardy!* music ends. "That's totally bogus!"

"Well, the bulk of the article talks

about who you are, how you came to live at the palace, and then speculates on what influence you might have on Georg. It doesn't actually say you're 'corrupt'—it's written more as a 'what if this person spending time with the prince is a corrupting influence?' and what that could mean for the country."

Like I'm going to single-handedly take down the monarchy of Schwerinborg? Puh-leeze.

"Can't we sue them? I mean, for making it sound like I'm some kind of junkie or something? All I did was walk into a bathroom with Georg. While I'll admit that hiding out in a men's room is not normal behavior, it doesn't mean I'm corrupting him."

I have no clue how suing a newspaper would work, but it's just wrong that they're able to write this when it's totally, completely false. I mean, could this hurt my chances of getting into a good college? Did they even think about that?

He takes another of his loud, deep breaths, then adjusts his tie, and stands up. "No. Litigation isn't an option at this point, so don't even think in that direction, Valerie. Besides, as bad as it sounds, you're not actually being accused of anything."

He gives me a look of sympathy, but thankfully he doesn't say "I told you so." "The next few days are probably going to be difficult, honey. I know you did nothing wrong, and the royal family knows that too. It's been a slow news week, so the papers are just itching for a good story and they're blowing this out of proportion. I think the best thing to do right now is to lie low and let it pass. Prince Manfred has a staff who handle public relations, and they'll advise us as to how we can speed up—"

The phone rings, and Dad reaches past me to grab it, saying that it might be the P.R. guys.

Instead, after a second, he hands the phone to me with a warning look to keep it short. "I'm going to Prince Manfred's offices and find out what's going on. I'll be back in a few minutes—don't go to school yet, and don't answer the phone."

I nod, hoping he'll boogie, because I am dying to know who's on the phone—

especially since he seems to think it's okay for me to talk to whoever it is.

As soon as Dad shuts the door, I say hello. And thankyou, thankyou, thankyou God, it's Georg. *Finally*.

"What's going on? I've been trying to reach you since yesterday!" I concentrate on my words so I don't sound desperate or ticked off, but I probably do, anyway. Mostly because I am.

"I know, I'm so sorry, Valerie. I wanted to call, but I couldn't."

"It's not your fault," I force myself to say in an understanding tone of voice that'd make Dad proud. "These things happen."

Well, I suppose they do if you're the girlfriend of a prince. But it's only been, like, three days, and already I'm sick and tired of everyone telling me they're *so sorry*. No wonder Princess Di was paranoid. I can't even imagine how many times during her life she must've had bad things happen, then everybody calling and apologizing to her after the fact.

And her prince didn't even love her like mine does.

"So what's going on?" I ask again, trying

to push the Princess Di images out of my head, since I'm clearly not anything like Princess Di was (rich, pretty, famous, etc.). "My dad just showed me the paper. Is that why you left school yesterday?"

"Yeah. Someone on the newspaper staff leaked the headline to our press office. The source wasn't certain it was going to run, but the P.R. guys wanted to talk to both me and my dad so they could formulate a response in case the story did go to press. That's why they sent the car to pick me up."

"Oh." So they'll work to defend him from nasty newspaper articles, but clearly not me. I suppose that's the way the world works, but having it flung in my face, even though I know he doesn't mean to, sucks major rocks.

I hear him messing with something, like he's flipping through the paper. "I'm really sorry, Valerie. I wanted to call you, but after the meeting, they drove me back to school for practice, and they were waiting to drive me home to talk to the P.R. guys again as soon as soccer let out. I didn't get a free minute the rest of the night. I didn't even get my homework done."

Whoa. He's neurotic about getting his homework done—almost as bad as I am. Though in his case, it's mostly 'cause he's afraid if he doesn't, it'll end up in the paper.

How's that for irony?

"Wow." I try to sound sympathetic, because I mostly am. "That totally blows."

"I got in around ten, then woke up at four a.m. so I could try to get my Trig homework finished, but I couldn't focus. All I wanted to do was call you because I was so worried the story would be in the paper. I was hoping it wouldn't be, since you and I both know there's nothing worth reporting. But one of the press office guys woke up my father just before five a.m. to let him know the story ran, and that it was worse than they'd thought. On the front page." He takes one of those deep Dad-like breaths. "I assume your father told you what the headline says?"

"Yeah. Apparently your dad translated for mine." And I'm guessing the conversation that followed wasn't particularly comfortable.

"Well, after I saw it, I really couldn't concentrate on Trig. I've been dying to call you ever since, but I wanted to wait until I knew for certain you were awake."

He sounds so sweet, and so Georg-ish, that I feel a major case of guilt. It's not his fault all this happened or that he couldn't call last night. I mean, it couldn't have been fun spending hours and hours holed up with a bunch of public relations geeks.

"Well, I'm really glad you called me," I tell him. "Even if it is with lousy news. I've been dying to hear your voice." His accent makes me melt, even if the rest of the world rots.

"I know. I wanted to hear your voice, too. I just don't want you to worry too much. The meetings went forever, but they all seem convinced it's going to blow over." He pauses for a sec, then adds, "That's the right way to use it, isn't it? Blow over? To mean something will go away soon?"

"Yep, you used it exactly the right way." His English is awesome, but sometimes he's not sure of certain phrases. It's incredibly cute, especially because he gets all embarrassed by it.

I really wish I could just shove the newspaper to the bottom of the recycling bin, curl up on my bed with Georg, and lie there. Just to be, and to not have to think about school or Steffi or reporters or anything else other than the way Georg talks to me, the way he smells when he's just taken a shower, or how much I love it when he wraps his arms around me and rubs my back.

And, for just a little while, I want to make him forget he's a prince. I want to let him hang out in my cold bedroom with the cracked wall and be normal—maybe watch TV or listen to some new CDs or something—and not have to worry about how every little thing he does gets hyper-analyzed by his family, the palace staff, all our classmates, and even the media.

"Are you going to school today?" I ask as I stuff my homework into my backpack, just in case. "Dad hasn't said whether he wants me to go yet or not, but if we both end up having to hide out inside the palace all day, our parents shouldn't mind if we do it together." Then at least one good thing could come out of all this crap.

"I don't know yet." He sounds a little cagey, and my alarms suddenly start going off. I get a really, really bad feeling. But instead of keeping quiet, I spout off and ask him if something else is wrong.

"It's nothing."

"It doesn't sound like nothing. Just tell me." I know, bad, bad move. Guys don't like being pushed to talk. Jules is always telling me that when a guy hedges with an answer, to let him hedge or you're not going to like the answer when he finally gives you one. But now I know he's not telling me something, and if I don't find out what it is, I'll go over the edge.

"My parents are worried about us, that's all. I don't think they were expecting things to get so exaggerated in the press."

"I don't think so either." I tell him about my conversation with Dad last night (apparently Dad didn't know about the possible newspaper article then, thank goodness) and about the one this morning. Georg tells me that his parents told him the same thing, basically: to lie low.

"So what did they say about us? Anything?"

He's quiet for a second too long. "Not much. But I think it'd be best if we cool it for a while."

"Cool it? What does that mean?"

"Well, you know what I mean."

No, I really have no clue. I close my eyes and lean back in my chair. "All right, then."

"Really? You're okay with it?"

What can I say if he won't tell me what he means by *it*? And I'm sure not going to ask him to clarify—*again*—since "cool it for a while" is certainly not going to work with my thought of hanging out together today, no matter what he means.

But what's really freaking me out is that I can't read whether he's okay with it—whatever *it* is he's proposing—from the way he asks.

And I can't tell whether "cool it" is his idea, his parents', or what. For all I know, it's the press office's, or the entire population of Schwerinborg's.

"I think my dad's back," I say, even though it's completely untrue. "Maybe we can talk later?"

"Definitely. I'll call you."

He sounds completely sincere, but I still wonder how many teenage angst movies I've seen where someone says, "I'll call you." It has to be a couple dozen. And in every single case, the guy never calls. It's code for something else, something not good.

I'm not sure, but I might've just been dumped.

To: Val@realmail.sg.com
From: NatNatNat@viennawest.edu
Subject: You really are . . .

SMOKING CRACK!

Okay, you KNOW I'm kidding. I know you'd never do drugs of any sort. But People of Earth to Valerie Winslow? Come in, Valerie Winslow! What's with you and the bathroom? And, let's see . . . hmmmm . . . THE PRINCE OF SCHWERINBORG???

I assume that this e-mail will bounce, because if your e-mail is working, you would have told me about this. RIGHT?!

I'm also assuming you haven't told Jules or Christie about this or they would have told me.

Or could it be you're keeping the world's

biggest secret because Jules is gonna kick your ass, since she has a thing for Georg? Or because Christie's gonna be completely bummed because she wants you to hook up with David, who's gorgeous AND totally into you, and what I saw makes it look like you're HOOKING UP WITH A PRINCE INSTEAD?

Lemme tell you, either way makes you a chickenshit.

So if this e-mail DOES go through, and you really have been keeping this from all of us, then I must ask: What kind of crack are you smoking?!

Curious, Natalie

P.S.: In normal person news, if you haven't heard, I'm grounded again. Bet you're just stunned (Hah!). Mom and Dad found out I got my tongue pierced. (I told you I got it pierced, right??) As you can guess, this did not go over well with Dr. Monschroeder, DDS. He gave me a half-hour lecture on the risks of fracturing my molars with the stud (doesn't "fracture my molar with a stud" sound vaguely kinky?), though he did stop short of reaching into my mouth to remove it. WHY does my father have to be a dentist? In any case, you can e-mail me whenever, 'cause I'm not leaving my room for the remainder of the decade.

To: Val@realmail.sg.com
From: CoolJule@viennawest.edu
Subject: Your Ass Kicking (Attachment: WashPost74692.jpg)

Oh, Val? Yeah, you. That ass kicking? It's imminent.

I CANNOT BELIEVE YOU!!!! Have you seen this picture? IT WAS IN THE WASHINGTON FREAKING POST!!

I think you really are doing drugs over there. That's the only way to explain 1) this picture; and 2) the fact you have not said ONE WORD to any of us about this.

Putting on my combat boots (and you can guess why),

Jules

P.S.: You know I got Schwerinborg right on the Geography exam last semester, right? The one where we were given the map of Europe and had to fill in the names of all the countries? I didn't even write down "Smorgasbord." So don't even

THINK I can't find your ass and kick it. I know where you live.

To: CoolJule@viennawest.edu
From: Val@realmail.sg.com
Subject: RE: Your Ass Kicking

Jules,

Okay, I have no idea why the *Washington Post* cares about any of this, but I'm telling you, it's NOTHING. It's just a picture they took of me outside school last week after I happened to walk to school with Georg—which is totally normal since we live in the same building, as you very well know because I TOLD YOU ABOUT IT.

And yes, I will now admit, there might have been a thing with Georg. Emphasis on MIGHT. And emphasis on HAVE BEEN.

And it just now happened. I haven't had a chance to tell anyone. Christie told me she was going to call, so I figured it was much better as a tell-it-on-the-phone thing.

I'm going to e-mail Christie and tell her to CALL. Okay? Will that save my butt from your combat boots for twenty-four hours or so?? Trust me, even if you could afford the airline ticket, you don't want to come to Schwerinborg.

Will explain everything as soon as possible, okay?

Love, Val

The *Washington Post*.

I CANNOT BELIEVE THIS!

I cannot even THINK about it. The picture Jules sent was apparently taken by the guy from *Majesty*, judging from the angle. It's not the same photo they ran in the paper here. And thankfully, the *Washington Post* is not calling me corrupt. I did a Google search on the article, and it's completely different than what was in the Schwerinborg paper. They just have three paragraphs saying that the prince of "tiny Schwerinborg" (and they also show it on the map, because of course no one in the States knows where Schwerinborg is except the twelve of us who actually got it correct on the Geography exam) might, MIGHT, be dating an American, and that we were seen sneaking into an empty restroom together.

It does mention that the press in Europe is speculating that Georg and I might have been doing drugs, but that the palace adamantly denies it. And the *Post* article states flat out that there's no evidence, in their words, that "either of these two teens, both of whom are honor roll students with spotless records, were dabbling in drugs."

They actually write about it like it's cool—the American-dates-European-prince-and-is-hounded-by-their-press angle, I suppose.

What's really pissing me off, though, isn't the newspapers, either here or in the States. It's not Jules's threat to put her boots to my butt, or Natalie (jokingly, I hope) telling me I must be smoking crack. It's the whole Georg thing.

Because, as I told Jules, and as the *Post* so eloquently states, it MIGHT have been a thing.

As in past tense.

As in, over before it began.

As in I am a complete and total idiot to have thought it meant a *thing*.

When I hung up after talking to Georg, I had a solid two hours to sit alone in my room and ignore the phone's constant ringing before I got distracted by e-mail (since, for once, I thought it'd be wise for me to listen to Dad and not answer the phone, even if every time it rang I was hoping it'd be Georg).

But the whole ignoring-the-phone thing was made much easier by a simple realization that hit me a few minutes after I hung up.

Georg said *I think it'd be best if we cool it for a while.* Not his parents. Not the press office.

I.

To use his own word, *definitely*, he's definitely not calling me again. This much I've figured out.

No wonder I've never had a boyfriend before. I clearly can't keep one for even a week. And come on——if it was him trying to reach me on the phone when it kept ringing and ringing, and if he really wanted to talk to me, then he'd try e-mailing or IM'ing me, too. But so far, nada on that front. Just all my buds from Virginia wanting a piece of me when I'm already as beaten down as I can get.

There's a light knock at my bedroom door. "Valerie?"

"Come on in, Dad." I'm so numb, I don't bother to move, even though I know I look completely lame. I've got one arm slung over my forehead, and I'm sprawled like one of those women who faints in Western movies after some guy dressed in black with really bad whiskey breath shoots the sheriff.

Except in my case, instead of having a totally hot cowboy crouching next to me, trying to loosen my corset so I can breathe, I'm just in jeans and an old sweater on my unmade bed, and I'm covered in Geometry homework.

As if on cue, my dad says, "I thought you finished your Geometry last night."

"I'm so freaking pathetic, I'm working ahead so I don't have to think about stuff."

My dad walks to the edge of my bed and shakes my foot, which he loves to do whenever I'm vegging out. "Don't use 'freaking,' Valerie. It sounds coarse."

I move my arm far enough off my face to look at him. He's clearly back to his old self. I'm not sure if that's good or bad for me.

"You have a package from your mother."

I push myself to a semi-sitting position, then look at the oversized, padded manila envelope with a horrible feeling of déjà vu. She warned me there'd be another self-help book, and this must be it. Dad can tell, too, because he's holding the thing toward me as if it's rat poison.

Kinda makes me wonder if he sort of blames Mom's giant collection of self-help books for her coming out of the closet. We both know that's not the case, obviously, but sometimes it sure feels that way. And there are days I think he wants to blame somebody, or something, for blindsiding him with the whole lesbian thing after nearly twenty years of marriage.

As bad as Mom's decision makes me feel, I know he has it much, much worse.

I pull the string tab on the side of the package, then look at Dad and hold up the book.

It's about cheese. No kidding. About who moved cheese. My mother is clearly getting back at me for making fun of her self-help book about moving cheese, because this is apparently the teen version. Gag.

I flip it over and look at the back cover. It's supposed to help me deal with change in my life. I don't think moving cheese around and having your brand-spankin'-new relationship (if that's what it was) dissected on the A.P. newswire are equivalent, but whatever.

At least, given the cheese angle, it might be more entertaining than the book she sent last week. That book tried to convince me that my problems were small stuff.

Hah.

I'm thinking no self-help book author ever had a mother come out of the closet and move in with a vegan. Or ever found herself forced to choose between living with her gay mom (and the vegan girlfriend) or moving to Schwerinborg, but that's just a wild guess on my part.

"Write your mother a nice e-mail to thank her," Dad says, though he looks like he's just thankful the book didn't come to him.

"I will," I grumble as I stuff the book back into the envelope.

"And while you're at it, you can tell her you'll be coming home next week for Winter Break."

Five

To: NatNatNat@viennawest.edu
From: Val@realmail.sg.com
Subject: I really am . . .

    1) NOT smoking crack, or anything else—not even emergency cigarettes;

    2) So not surprised you did the tongue-stud thing;

    3) Also not surprised about your being grounded (um, DUH, Natalie—did you honestly think you wouldn't be?); and

    4) Sitting in my room in the ice palace at this very moment, printing off the confirmation for a Lufthansa airlines e-ticket to Virginia, courtesy of my father.

In other words, I will be there next week for Winter Break. Please hide Jules's combat boots, if you can. I swear I will explain everything when I get there.

Love, Val

P.S.: Is Christie gone or something? She hasn't e-mailed. Also, she was supposed to call but never did.

Spin control.

This is how my dad explains the fact that I am now on a plane, taxiing (is that really a verb?) toward the Jetway at Dulles International Airport.

Apparently, after his conference with Prince Manfred and Princess Claudia, Dad worried that things might get out of hand in the press. (I immediately asked if they could possibly get any worse, and Dad assured me they could. He even offered several hypothetical examples that convince me his protocol-wired brain is actually quite warped.)

So for the week of Winter Break, they—they being my dad, Georg's parents, and all the suits in public relations at the palace—thought it would be a grand idea for me to get outta town and let the P.R. office deal with the press. Frankly, I'd rather stay in Schwerinborg to avoid 1) Jules's ass-kicking; 2) dealing with Mom; and 3) making things even worse with Georg.

When I complained to Dad about not being consulted, he told me that I'm fifteen and should get over it already—though he said it in a more formal, dad-ish way that made it hard for me to argue against.

My dad explained that the P.R. guys would accidentally but on purpose leak a story about how I would spend my vacation in the United States with family (making me sound very goody-goody and non-junkie-like), while Georg and some of the other guys from his year eleven class go skiing in Zermatt. Of course they would also accidentally but on purpose mention that Georg would be stopping to visit kids in hospitals on the way to and from Switzerland. All that nicey-nice prince stuff.

This is evidently what media types refer to as spin control: attempting to change or control the direction that a particular story will take in the press.

So after the week from hell at school—where Steffi gave me these *I'm so so sorry* (NOT!) looks, Ulrike walked around with a horrible guilty expression plastered to her perfect face, Maya simply avoided me, and my dad drove me to school so the reporters would have to leave me alone—Prince Manfred had his limousine take me from the palace to the Freital airport. Dad gave me a hundred bucks just in case, then sent me off. And now here I am, back in the States, in what must be the world's most butt-ugly airport.

Controlling spin.

According to my father, the hope is that the press will believe that: 1) Georg and I are not together (which might actually be true, depending on what "cool it" means); and/or 2) whether we're together or not, we are good little kids and not the type to use drugs.

Although if anything will drive me to smoke weed, I decide it has to be the sight just past airport security. Yee-gads.

Mom brought Gabrielle.

I kind of figured she would, but seeing them together makes me want to hork up the airplane food. Don't they realize I'm suffering enough already?!

"Val-er-eeeee!" My mom is jumping up and down and waving to make sure I recognize her in the crowd, as if her image hasn't been burned on my brain from birth.

I wave back, hoping it'll shut her up, even though I'm disappointed to see that she obviously still thinks her buzz cut is a good idea—she looks freshly shorn. I'd really been hoping she'd grow her hair back out. No woman my mother's age—let alone a woman named Barbara—should wear her hair that short. Does she not own a mirror? Has she not seen a recent copy of *Glamour* or *Vogue*—or, geez, even *Good Housekeeping*?

Once I pass through security, she gives me this monster hug. I suddenly realize that I've missed her hugs, even though she always hugs me so tight it crushes my shoulders because she's one of those super lovey-dovey moms. You know, the kind who hugs you as if she thinks you're never,

ever going to hug her again, every single time.

"Oh, Valerie, honey! I'm so glad to have you home!"

"Thanks." I know I should tell her I'm glad to be here, but even though I've had almost a week to get used to the idea, I still can't decide. I mean, Jules refuses to reconsider her threats to do me bodily harm (with Natalie's full support) and that's the least of my problems. Four e-mails to Christie have gone completely unanswered, and all of my IMs have been ignored, which is a Very Bad Thing.

Even worse, Gabrielle is looking at me with this dopey, mom-ish smile, and I just know she's going to tell me how much she's looking forward to spending this week getting to know me better. I've gotta give her props for hanging back and trying to give me and Mom a little space to hug and say hello, but when I give Gabrielle a polite smile—because it's the nice thing to do and I know it's what Dad would expect—I still feel like a total faker doing it. Especially when she gives me this *I'm so excited you like me* look.

Blond freak. I mean, ICK.

"I'm really happy to see you, Mom," I finally say, focusing on her. And it's no lie—I am glad to see her. Just not her haircut or her girlfriend, particularly. I mean, she's still my mom and I still love her, even if I feel like I don't understand her anymore.

I try to act all happy and smiley as we pick up my suitcase from the carousel, and the two of them ask me about the flight and whether or not I'm hungry. But by the time we're walking out to Mom's green Toyota SUV, I'm only half-listening. My bullshit detector's going off, and I can't pinpoint why. Since it's pretty finely tuned, even when I'm tired and grumpy, I figure I'm better off just keeping my mouth shut and watching the two of them.

Or not watching. As Gabrielle puts my suitcase in the back of the SUV and we all climb in, I figure it out: The two of them haven't stood within five feet of each other since I came through security.

This has to be planned. I mean, given how intense they were with each other in the weeks before I moved to Schwerinborg, they must have discussed ahead of time how to act around me. Decided not to hold hands or do anything mushy.

While I know they're doing it so I won't freak out, it's having the opposite effect. It's making me wonder what they're hiding. What they're really like together on an everyday basis. And what they think of my being here.

I'm an intruder in my own mother's car.

I grab an elastic out of my purse, yank my hair back into a ponytail, then turn and stare out the window. It feels bizarre to be back in the States, even though I've only been gone a few weeks. I've lived in Virginia all my life, but only now am I noticing how wide the roads are and how loud people are when speaking to one another compared to how they speak in Europe. And in Virginia, everything is spread out. We have to drive five miles to the mall, and three to a movie theater. School is nowhere near walking distance for 99 percent of the students.

At the palace, on the other hand, I can walk to anything. School. Shops. Whatever. Even my boyfriend's—assuming I have one. And lots of Europe seems to be that way. City-ish and walkable.

As we slide from one lane into another and the trees and houses of suburbia flash by out my window, I try to adjust mentally to being home. The air even feels different when I crack my car window, and when Mom turns on the radio to my favorite station, the sound of American English and the obnoxious commercials make my new life with Dad feel very far away.

And it makes Georg feel far away too.

I know I shouldn't be so hung up on him, especially when I'm fairly certain I've been dumped, but I can't help it. All week long he's all I could think about. I saw him sneaking looks at me in the halls at school and he didn't seem openly hostile or anything. He even shot me a little smile once when no one was looking—just enough to make me keep my hopes up. On the other hand, he never once approached me—let alone e-mailed me—and I sure as hell wasn't going to walk up to him.

I just wish I knew whether his whole avoidance thing is part of the plan for spin control—I mean, is he avoiding me because his parents say he has to, and maybe it's a temporary thing? 'Cause that would explain the looks and the smile. Or is it because he's figured out for himself that it's not worth it to date me and he wants to extract himself from our relationship while he has a good excuse? Either way, as I lean my head back against the headrest and stare out the window, I feel very much alone.

The pathetic part is that I can't help but wonder if he feels alone too. I mean, if he wants to break up with me, fine. Well, not fine. But it'd be a hell of a lot better if he'd just freakin' say it. Just flat out end it. Otherwise, this whole living in limbo will slowly eat me alive.

But part of me thinks he doesn't. Part of me is convinced that what we have is special, and "cool it" really means that we have to stay away from each other awhile so we can be together later—which, in a way, is totally romantic and totally believable, coming from Georg.

"Valerie, did you hear me?" Mom turns in her seat and frowns at me as she angles the car down the exit ramp and through the streets of Vienna.

"Sorry, Mom. Guess I'm tired." I didn't sleep well last night (go figure), and the flight has my body clock all screwed up. I left Schwerinborg at noon their time, and now it's two p.m., Virginia time. I think that means eight or nine p.m. in Schwerinborg, but my brain's just not operational.

"I suppose so. You haven't said a word about where we're headed."

"Home, right?" I lean forward and don't see anything unusual. Then it hits me: We're headed toward MY home. The home where I grew up. Where I lived with Mom and Dad until Mom left to move in with Gabrielle. I'm so used to driving this direction from the airport that I forgot we weren't supposed to come this way anymore. That we should have gone to Mom's new place—the apartment she shares with Gabrielle.

"I thought you might like to see your friends for a while before we go to the apartment. And this gives me a chance to water your father's plants and pay the bills."

"Oh. Okay." I still think it's strange

that Dad is having Mom look after his stuff while he's away, but he insists they're still friends despite the divorce and that he's more comfortable with her taking care of things than asking a neighbor or one of his buddies.

Geez, but I hope I never get divorced and have to deal with this level of weirdness in my life.

"Um, I didn't tell my friends when I was getting in," I tell Mom. "I mean, they know it's today, but they don't know what time unless you told them."

"Of course I did," Mom says, and her voice is just overflowing with happy-happy-happy. "Julia, Natalie, and Christie all agreed to come over. They should be at the house about twenty minutes after we get there. I wanted to give you a little more time, so you could shower or take a nap if you wanted, but your flight came later than scheduled."

"That's okay." For one, the girls have seen me smelly and gross before. For two, even if I look like I just crawled out of the Potomac, they aren't going to notice. They're going to be far, far more interested in telling me off than in whether I've loofa-hed in the last twenty-four hours.

And despite what Mom thinks, Christie probably won't show. It's completely unlike her to ignore e-mail. And I know the e-mail thing is no accident, because she was way worked up to call me, all the way over in Schwerinborg, and on her mother's dime, too. In exchange, her mother made her promise to be nice to her Tennessee cousins for a solid week when they came to visit. She even made Christie take them to the Smithsonian and all the typical Washington tourist sites.

Christie even went along on the freaking White House tour, which she's totally sick of, so I know she really wanted to talk.

But after the Georg thing hit the *Washington Post*, she didn't even bother to pick up the phone, so it doesn't take superior insight to guess what her attitude toward me must be. She's feeling totally betrayed, and I don't blame her. She's the best friend I've ever had, and so hiding all this from her is pretty huge.

"You don't look very excited to see everyone, honey." My mom is looking at me in the rearview mirror, and I feel bad because I know she went to a lot of trouble to get everyone to come over. Five bucks says she even went shopping this morning and picked up treats of some sort from Giant. (Well, now that she's living with Gabrielle, I guess they'd get groceries from Whole Foods instead—and I'm guessing Whole Foods does not carry Ho Hos, which Mom always used to keep in the pantry because they're Jules's fave.)

"I'll be fine once I can eat and sleep a little," I say as we pull into the driveway. Thankfully, no one's beaten us here, so as soon as I break away from Mom and the freak, I dump my stuff in my room— which has to be ten degrees warmer than my room in the palace even though no one's even been living here—and take a quickie shower.

Why I even bother, I have no idea.

Surprise, surprise. When I walk back into my bedroom in one of my mom's old ratty robes, there's Christie, sitting on my bed. She's the same beautiful self she's always been, and I instantly feel horribly, terribly guilty for keeping so much from her.

"Hey." The word comes out froglike— probably because my quickie shower ended up taking nearly half an hour. (I think my brain needed to soak.) "I didn't think you'd come."

"Well, I did." She doesn't even bother to stand up. She's not visibly mad or visibly happy, just blah—which means she's about as angry as she can get.

"I guess we need to talk." I sound like a total dork, but we've never had a fight before, ever, so I don't know how to deal with Angry Christie. She's usually the peacemaker in our group. "I didn't mean to piss you off, really," I tell her. "You're my best friend. Ever."

"So you keep secrets from me?"

"No—"

"Funny, because I swear the *Washington Post* knows more about your life than I do."

I unwrap the towel from my head and toss it over my desk chair. "Okay, I did keep secrets from you. But I didn't mean to. I was just confused, and I needed time to absorb everything. And"—I look her in the eye, which doesn't help matters, because she still looks very blah and unreadable, which, for Christie, is hard to do—"I didn't think you'd understand."

"What I don't understand is what's downstairs." She lowers her voice and points toward the door. "Who is that woman? She's not a neighbor, so I thought she might be from your mom's book club or something, but they don't look like book club buddies to me."

Oh, crap. How could this not occur to me on the ride home?

GABRIELLE IS HERE.

And I can't lie to Christie. Not with everything else. She'd never speak to me again, and right now, I just can't handle having her hate me. "Are Jules or Natalie here?" I ask.

"Not yet. I came early so I could see you alone. Good thing I did, too." Christie leans forward, and she actually looks concerned. "There's a lot more you're not telling me than the fact you're getting busy with some European prince—isn't there?"

I open the curtains partway and stand near the window—not to flash the neighborhood, but so I have warning when Jules and Natalie show up—then I look back at Christie. She's probably figured it out, but even if she hasn't, I have to tell her. "'That woman' . . . is named Gabrielle. And Gabrielle is my mother's new girlfriend."

"Girlfriend." Her voice is dead level, but I can tell what she wants to know.

"Yeah. And so you don't have to ask—she's that kind of girlfriend."

"You are freaking kidding me! Get OUT!" Her voice is low, but I glance toward the door, anyway, to make sure Mom and Gabrielle don't hear. "Your mother . . . is she . . . does she think she's *gay?*"

"Yeah. She is."

All of a sudden, I feel myself getting teary, which I completely did not expect. I manage to hold it in, but when I hear my own voice, I sound like I'm about to completely lose it. "That's why she and my dad are getting divorced. My mom decided—or admitted to herself or however you want to describe it—that she's gay, and announced over dinner one night that she didn't want to stay married to my dad. That it wasn't anything either of us had done, and that nothing would change her mind, it's just that she—and these were her exact words—*needed to be true to herself*, even though she knew it was going to be hard on me and Dad."

Instantly, Christie comes over to the window and gives me a hug. And then I can't help it. The waterworks start, and I realize how hard it's been not to be able to tell my friends—Christie, most of all—what's been going on with Mom and Dad.

"That's terrible, Valerie," she says in a whisper, right next to my ear. "I never in a million years would have guessed. I'm so sorry."

For once, I don't care that someone's saying she's sorry—probably because this time I know it's heartfelt. And, of course, that thought makes me snarfle right into Christie's shoulder. "She dumped my dad right in front of me, Christie. It was so awful. I mean, I was beyond blown away, but Dad . . . the look on his face scared me. It was like she'd died or something."

"Why didn't you tell me, Val? It's been weeks and weeks!"

"I didn't think you'd understand.

Telling you guys about the divorce was bad enough. And I felt so stupid." I'm totally blubbering now, though it's a restrained kind of blubbering, since I don't want Mom to hear any of this. I'm sure Christie thinks I've lost my mind, but I don't care anymore.

Christie lets me go because she's getting teary too. She reaches over to the top of my desk and grabs a tissue. They look a little dusty, since no one's been in the house for a month, but she shoves it toward me, anyway, then takes one for herself. "Why would you feel stupid?"

"Because I didn't know. I mean, I had no clue. How could I not know my own mother is a lesbian?"

Geez, I hate how that word sounds coming out of my mouth—like I think being a lesbian is a horrid thing. In my gut, though, I don't believe that. It is what it is, and I really do believe Mom when she says it's just who she is—that this wasn't a choice she made. But still.

"I just—I didn't even see the divorce coming, Christie. I actually thought my mother was kidding at first. Who ends a twenty-year marriage on a Wednesday night over Kraft Mac and Cheese?"

"But she wasn't kidding."

"Nope." I snorf into the tissue. I'm sure I look like hell, especially in this nasty robe and with my hair all wet, but whatever. "I'm pretty sure she'd already hooked up with Gabrielle when she made her little announcement, because they had an apartment lined up within days. And then it was so hard telling you guys that my parents were getting divorced that I couldn't bring myself to tell you what was really going on, that it was so much more than that, and—"

"Val. Hey, Valerie." Christie pegs me with a look, one that speaks volumes, letting me know she totally, completely gets it. She knows I'm dying inside, because my mother not only has this whole other existence I had no clue about and feelings toward other women I never could have predicted, but she also cheated on my dad. "It's okay," she tells me. "I mean, it's not okay, but I'm on your side here. I just wish you'd felt like you could tell me."

"Me too."

"Oh, man!" Christie's eyes get huge. "Your mom must think that I already know. And Jules and Natalie, too. That's why she invited us all over."

I swallow really hard and try to wipe my face clean with the tissue. I so do not want Jules and Natalie to see me looking this way.

"I didn't even think about Gabrielle being here until you asked about her just now. I'm having a major brain fart kind of day." Then I get a panicky thought. "There's no way I can tell Jules and Natalie. I just can't."

"Then don't. At least not today. But you should, at some point. They're your friends too. Give them a little credit, okay?" Christie glances out the window, then turns toward my dresser. "Sit. Dry your hair. I'll get you some clothes."

"Thanks. I swear, you're the best friend in the world."

"Keep that in mind next time your life falls apart."

As she tosses me a pair of old jeans, then opens my closet to search for a top, I ask her how she thinks I should explain

Gabrielle, since the freak's not going anywhere before Nat and Jules come over.

"Well, maybe they won't notice. They'll think she's just a girlfriend or something." She looks back at me, and the tiniest smile pulls at the edge of her mouth. We can't help it. We both crack up.

"You're awful, Christie. But in a really, really good way. Seriously—thanks for being cool with all of this."

She does a little hip shake. "I'm always cool."

"You two are awfully quiet. Is everything cool up there?" Mom hollers from the bottom of the stairs.

"Yes!" we both answer, then crack up again.

"Natalie and Julia should be here any minute," Mom calls up. "You should all come down and have something to eat. I even bought some Ho Hos for Julia!"

"Okay!" We both yell back.

"Well, that proves she's still the same mom you had before," Christie says as she picks out a black V-neck sweater from the closet. "She remembered Jules's heart attack in a box."

I let out a deep breath as I start to brush my hair out. "Yeah, I guess."

"Look, if Jules or Natalie ask, you can just lie and tell them she's from the PTA or something—well, as long as neither of them ask right in front of your mom or Gabrielle."

I give Christie a look that says, YOU would lie? Christie is pretty much incapable of falsehood, and everyone knows it. She's that disgustingly pure.

"Just for today," she says. "And if they do ask in front of them, I'll just mention Prince Georg and or the *Washington Post* and that'll solve the problem. They'll forget all about Gabrielle."

"Great." I roll my eyes. "And about Georg, it's a really long story—"

"I figured, and I haven't forgiven you for not telling me. Plus, I'm still dying to know what in the world is going on. You'd better tell me soon, too, because whether you like it or not, you're going out with me and Jeremy tonight. I already asked your mom if it's okay."

"I don't want to be a third wheel. I'm here all week, so we can do it another night if—"

"You won't be a third wheel." Her blue eyes light up, and I know what's coming even before she says it. "David's coming too. That's why you have to fill me in on whatever you have or don't have going on with His Royal Gorgeousness. Before we go."

"Christie!" I can't possibly go out with them. Not when the whole Georg thing is unresolved. And I'm going to need to explain the spin control concept to Christie 'cause I'm thinking this is a no-no, even if I wanted to go.

As if there weren't enough other reasons to say *no way in hell* to a night out with David—reason number one being I'm David's Armor Girl, not a potential princess.

"Are you going out with Georg? You can't possibly be." Her eyes lock with mine, and in that instant I know she knows. She's been my best bud way too long not to read me. "Omigosh. Valerie, you are. YOU ARE!!!"

"Actually, it's not really—"

"Have you guys been fooling around? Are you committed? Is it serious?!"

I tick off the answers to her questions

on my fingers. "Yes, I don't know, and I don't know, but——"

"Then you're coming out tonight. We're going to dinner, and I have tickets for all four of us to a nine o'clock movie. You have to come. You have to give David a chance to talk to you. Please? For me?"

"Does David think this is a date?" I can't go on a date—a real, official *date*— can I?

Even if I've dreamed about David Anderson asking me out since I was learning about two-plus-two and reading books like *Dick and Jane* and *A Duck Is a Duck*, it just feels like it'd be wrong.

But holy smokes. A date with DAVID ANDERSON?! The most gorgeous guy in the whole school? The guy who makes Paul Walker look only sorta cute in comparison?

The guy whose yearbook picture I photocopied and then taped up next to my bed, where he stayed hidden behind my pillows for over a year just so I could see him every night before I went to sleep?

Okay, I destroyed that photo in a moment of exceedingly good judgment before I went to Schwerinborg, deciding

I'd been a total obsessive freak to copy his picture in the first place, but still . . .

NO. No, no, no. It's just wrong. Wrong, wrong, wrong, wrong, wrong!!

"It's casual. Sort of," Christie says as I pull on my jeans and the sweater. "Let's just see what happens after you two talk."

"This is a bad idea. Seriously."

"Jules and Natalie are here," she says, looking out the window. "Jules's mom is already backing out of the driveway. And hey, Jules really did wear her combat boots!"

I'm thinking, for the first time, that this might actually be a good thing.

If Jules kicks me hard enough, I won't have to go tonight.

On the other hand, a little tiny part of me wants to go, just to satisfy my curiosity.

"Shoot me now," I tell Christie. "Just get it over with."

"She's not that mad at you," Christie says, making a squished-up face (which is hard for her to do). "She's always this way. I think she's mostly interested in finding out what's up with Georg. A little jealous, but mostly just interested."

"No, I meant shoot me before we have

to go out tonight. I can't believe you did this without talking to me first!"

Christie levels her worst stare at me. It's not that threatening if you don't know her, because she can't look violent even if she tries. But I know she's serious. "Like you not talking to me before you hook up with Prince Charming? Hell-o?"

At that moment, I hear Jules yelling up the stairs, and Mom introducing Gabrielle to Natalie.

Oh, crap.

Six

I think I have said about ten extremely heartfelt thank yous to God in the last hour that both Jules and Natalie are the type of people who become oblivious to everything but themselves when they're ticked off.

While their occasional self-centeredness is usually an annoying trait, today it's good.

BECAUSE I JUST SAW MY MOTHER KISS ANOTHER WOMAN!

Okay, it was on the cheek. And it was when she thought none of us were looking— which I can understand, because we were all sitting in the eating area and she and Gabrielle were in the kitchen, which is nearby, but not in the direct line of vision from most of the table.

When IT happened, Jules was tearing open the Hostess box and Natalie was griping about how she's only allowed out for two hours, and *only* because I'm home and her parents are granting her a "special break" from the maximum security block (aka, her bedroom) because she's still in trouble for the tongue piercing. And Christie chose the seat facing away from the kitchen, so she saw nothing. But *still*.

This is beyond bizarre. I mean, Mom and Gabrielle looked all cheery when we came downstairs and plunked down at the table. The two of them stood in the kitchen while Christie yakked about Natalie's tongue piercing and Jules argued that it's probably no worse for Natalie's health than ignoring the trans-fat content of her own beloved Ho Hos—despite all of Dr. Monschroeder's dire warnings about Natalie's risk of breaking a molar or getting an infection.

Mom and Gabrielle were both sipping herbal tea and smiling in that parental sort of way that translates to *I'm so glad my kid is happy in life and has such wonderful friends.* Then Gabrielle turned and said something to Mom very quietly about the Ho Hos—probably agreeing with Jules's trans-fat comment—and Mom's smile got even bigger. Then Mom leaned over and kissed Gabrielle on the cheek—the exact same way she used to kiss Dad when they were having a happy-warm-fuzzy family moment.

For a moment, I just froze. I could not believe what I just witnessed.

It didn't make me angry or anything. It wasn't even that gross (which you'd *think*). It was just . . . *weird*.

But now I can't focus on the conversation around me. I keep sneaking peeks into the kitchen to see if they're going to do it again.

Or if they'll do something else. I mean, what *do* they do in public? I haven't been around to see. Do they hold hands when they go to the movies? Are they lovey-dovey in the grocery store?

I AM NOT GOING TO THINK ABOUT THIS!!

It's all just so wrong, them doing

whatever it is they do, and even worse, my thinking about it so much.

"Valerie?" Mom sets down her teacup and leans on the counter to catch my attention. "Didn't you have something to show your friends up in your room?"

I grunt an uh-huh, because I think she means the presents I brought from Schwerinborg. Dad, ever the protocol expert, bought some beautiful bracelets for everyone in a really pricey Freital jewelry shop. (And yes, I wanted to do it myself, out of principle, but I couldn't leave the palace without the press following me. And I couldn't have afforded what Dad spent, anyway, so who am I to gripe?)

But part of me also wonders if Mom is making her suggestion because she wants time alone with Gabrielle. Though why, when they've had the last few weeks without anyone else around, is beyond me.

Maybe they feel like they're on their honeymoon or something, now that Mom and Dad are separated and Mom's officially filed for divorce.

"Yeah, let's go upstairs so we can talk,

Val!" Jules says after licking the last of the chocolate off a Ho Ho wrapper. She not-so-subtly punctuates the remark by bashing one of her boots into my instep. "We have a ton to catch up on!"

Natalie sticks out her tongue and bugs her eyes at me.

"Okay, that is beyond disgusting," I tell her, even though Natalie just being Natalie makes me feel a better, in a bass-ackward sort of way. "I mean, OUCH."

"Ouch is right," Jules says under her breath, but as we all get up, Christie glares at her, making it clear that she not only heard Jules's comment but that she wants Jules to lay off until she gets the whole story.

Thankyou, thankyou, thankyou, Christie.

"So, things haven't changed one bit with you since the last time we were all in here," Jules says in a totally fake but funny voice once we get into my room and the door's shut. "You're exactly the same old Val we all know and love. You're open, honest—"

"I get it already." I don't even bother to sound apologetic. Although, with the honesty thing, I wonder whether Jules is referring to Georg, my mom, or both. I'm not sure which topic sucks more to deal with, but since I know they know about Georg—at least as much as they read in the *Post*—I figure I should lead with that. "Look, I really didn't mean to hide anything from you guys. But everything happened so fast."

"You're telling me." Jules fiddles with my hairbrush, then sets it back down on top of my dresser. "I can't believe your mom moved on already. I mean, the divorce can't be final. It's way too fast. Have they even filed yet?"

Natalie sprawled on my bed when we came in, but at Jules's question, she sits up straight and stares at her. "What are you talking about?"

I hate that Jules is such an expert on the whole marriage-divorce thing. And not just because it sucked to be her as a kid, since her parents got divorced when we were all in third grade. Her mom remarried the next year, but that marriage blew up the summer before we started sixth grade. Her parents then remarried—each other, of all people—when we were in eighth grade.

On top of the whole why-won't-my-parents-just-settle thing ruining her elementary school years, the experience made Jules way too perceptive about how adults handle relationships. Well, at least perceptive enough to tell that my mom and Gabrielle aren't just friends.

I make myself face Jules's stare-down. "It was obvious the minute you walked in the door, huh? I should have known you'd figure it out."

"WHAT was obvious?" Natalie demands. I know she suspects what we're hinting at now, but she can't bring herself to believe it. She looks at Christie, whose eyes are huge, because Christie's in awe of Jules for figuring it out so easily. Natalie looks at Jules for confirmation, then to me. "No way. NO WAY! Are you serious?"

"Dead serious. Unfortunately."

"Oh, wow. Your mom's a dyke now? Gay?" She pauses for a second before asking, "What *is* the proper word? 'Lesbian,' I guess? Unless she's bi—?"

"Well, definitely not 'dyke,'" I tell her, though I'm really not sure about any of this stuff either. "I think 'lesbian's the most PC, but 'gay' works, too. And no, I don't think she's bisexual. Just gay."

"That completely blows. I was hoping I was wrong." Jules turns my desk chair around and sits in it backward. "Just for that, I completely forgive you for keeping the Prince Georg thing to yourself. There will be no retribution whatsoever. The boots are off."

"Gee," I say, and I can't help but grin at her. "My ass and I both thank you."

I can tell that Jules and Natalie really do feel bad for me, which wasn't at all what I expected. I know, I know, they're my *buds,* and I should trust them. But this isn't something any of us have dealt with before. Jules's situation was completely different, plus you never *really* know where most people stand on the whole gay issue until they're face-to-face with it, no matter what they've said in the past. It's just too dicey for most people to handle.

"How's your dad dealing with it?" Christie asks. "I hope he's okay."

She's always been really tight with my parents, so this can't be easy news for her, either. She's been coming over to my house to hang out and for sleepovers since we were really little.

"He doesn't talk about it much." I give them all a half-shrug. "I mean, he's probably got plenty to say, but he wants me and Mom to stay close. I think he's afraid if he gets negative about the situation, it's going to make me more ticked off at Mom than I already am."

"About her being gay?" Nat asks.

"No. I'm not mad about that." I don't think. "Though I'm not *happy* about it, you know? I'm more mad that she was lying to us all this time."

"Did she know she's . . . well, you know. Do you think she's known all along?" Christie asks.

I can tell from the way she's scrunching her nose that ever since Christie arrived and discovered the truth, all this has been slowly percolating in her head. And now that I think about it, she was pretty quiet when we were having our Ho Ho time downstairs.

She's probably been thinking about all the times Mom has seen her naked, or at least in her bra and underwear. Like when we've gone to the day spa as a treat from Mom, or when Mom stuck her head in my room when Christie and I were changing clothes to go running or to a dance or whatever.

Or maybe Christie's more enlightened than most people, and instead, she's thinking about all the other stuff that had me going berserk the first week or so after I found out. I mean, my mom declaring she's gay is as close as it gets to Christie having her own mother come out of the closet.

Well, except Christie's mom used to be a nun (before she met Christie's dad). And Christie's pretty religious herself. So maybe she's just thinking that my mom's a horrible sinner, and how awful it is for me that my mom might go to hell.

Whoa. I hope that's not what Christie thinks.

I flop onto the bed next to Natalie. Careful to choose just the right words, I say, "I dunno. I think she was lying to herself as much as to me and Dad about her orientation."

I catch Christie's eye, just for reassurance, and I realize that at least part of my hunch about Christie's feelings is dead on. While I can't tell whether she thinks Mom is committing some huge sin, as far as she's concerned, we're in this together. My bad news is her bad news.

I am so so so so glad she's my best friend. No matter what her belief system tells her, she's at least going to *try* to be understanding.

"You're angry because you think your mom cheated on your dad," Jules says before Christie does. "Otherwise, how could she have hooked up with Miss Thang down there so quickly—right?"

I just nod. The whole room suddenly fills with this whispered chorus of *I'm so sorry*s and *oh that's terrible*s, and I can't help but not want to hear it anymore.

"Can we talk about something else?" I ask, even though I know what they're going to want to talk about. "Not that I'm blowing you guys off, but another topic would sure make me feel better. I'm sick of thinking about the whole my-mother-is-gay thing right now."

"Hmmmm . . . Georg the Gorgeous?" Jules gets a wicked grin on his face. "You know if he lived within a twenty-mile radius of here, he'd be mine."

"Yeah, yeah, yeah," I say, as Natalie tosses one of my pillows at Jules's head and tells her to give me a break. So I fill them in on everything—starting with my meeting Georg and our flirting a little, then our date to his dad's fancy event. I tell them about making out in the palace garden and in the public restroom, though I try to be casual about that part, as if I've kissed lots of guys and making out with Georg that night is just another part of the story and not the absolute best, most mind-blowing thing that's happened to me in my life.

I also tell them about the cigarettes (that we were NOT smoking) and about my dad catching us. I finish up with all the stuff about the *Majesty* reporter, the bizzaro conversation at lunch with Ulrike and her buddies, the photos in the European papers, and the entire concept of spin control.

"So you don't know if you and Georg

are together or not?" Christie's incredulous as she asks this. "You *have* to have a gut instinct—I mean, you don't even have a hint, like from his tone of voice or anything?"

"Nope. Not a clue." Was she not listening? I mean, I suppose I could tell them about the little smile he gave me in the hall at school, but then they'd tell me I was giving him credit where credit's not due, or they'd tell me I'd imagined it—either way, I don't want to hear it.

"How well do you really know him?" Natalie asks. "Not to be harsh on the guy, because it does sound like he's pretty damned incredible, and I mean, he's a freaking *prime*. But how can you not know if you're together?"

"Look, things were kind of crazy right before I left. How many relationships have you been in where the entire staff of a freaking *press office* wants to weigh in on every little thing you do? It changes things."

Not that I have any basis of comparison, and neither do they. Jules and Natalie are both short-term-relationship types.

Their M.O. with guys is to go out, make out, and then get out.

And Christie's had one—ONE—boyfriend. They've been together for quite a while now, which explains why she responds: "But if you two really like each other, and want to be together, that shouldn't matter. I mean, look at Jeremy and me. If we're separated, like when he goes to running camps in the summer to train for cross-country season, we're still a couple. We don't have to talk about it or anything—it's a given."

"So you guys are telling me that 'cool it' means Georg has dumped me?"

They all look at one another, then Jules shrugs. "Maybe. I mean, we weren't there, and since you left us out of the loop it's not like we can give you a fair assessment."

"What I think," Natalie tells me in a very deliberate tone, "is that you need to decide whether *you* want to be with *him*. That's what really matters."

I frown at her, because she's sounding like my mother—or, more accurately, like one of Mom's self-help gurus. "I can't be with him if he doesn't want me, so I don't know that that's helpful. I mean, what if I *do* want him, but he doesn't want me?"

"Then forget him," Jules mutters, "and I'll have a crack at the boy."

I ignore her. In the most unemotional and firm voice I can manage, I say, "Well, we can debate it all day long, but there's no point. I won't know anything for sure until I get back to Schwerinborg and Georg and I can sort it all out."

Assuming the spin control plan actually works and we're allowed to have more than a five-minute face-to-face conversation alone, that is.

"That's not true," Christie cuts in. "Just go out with David while you're here. I bet you decide pretty quickly whether Georg is really the guy for you once you're out with David. Even if Georg is a prince and you think he 'gets' you."

Right. I can tell what she's really saying is: 1) Georg *doesn't* get me, or he would have known to explain "cool it"—or to not even say "cool it" in the first place; and 2) David *does* get me, so who cares if Georg does or not, since I've been crushing on David practically my whole life?

"I agree with Christie," Natalie says. "What can it hurt?"

Well, it can hurt Georg. But I'm not going to say that aloud because it's clear to me that they're all in David's corner.

"Okay, fine. I'll go out with David." I point a finger at Christie. "But it is NOT a date. Casual really has to mean casual, okay? Make that crystal clear to David and to Jeremy. I still believe I'm the Armor Girl."

"You're wrong," Christie says. "But you can wait and see for yourself."

To: Val@viennawest.edu
From: GvE@zasucafe.ch
Subject: Are you there?

I know this is your old e-mail address from home, but I thought I'd try to send to it on the off-chance you'd get it.

I'm at an Internet café in Zermatt—I managed to get over here from my hotel without anyone from the press following me. I think I can safely send you a message, but you know how that goes, so I'll keep this basic.

I just wanted you to know I meant what I said after the dinner. The way things happened afterward, I wasn't sure you'd know that anymore.

Don't respond—this is only a temporary address—but I promise we'll talk as soon as possible after we both get back. I'll find a way. Even if I have to sneak out at midnight to do it.

G—

I forgot how completely, totally, unequivocally gorgeous and witty David is. I had a crush on him for nearly a *decade* for a very, very good reason.

I keep peeking over at him in the next chair, watching him watch the movie (and hoping he doesn't see me doing it), and thinking about how his surfer-blond hair and smooth, just-tanned-even-in-the-winter skin makes him look like he belongs in a movie himself.

And speaking of the movie . . . yeah, it's

Heath Ledger. And it's one of those historical dramas. Christie KNOWS I get all hot and bothered by Heath wearing a fancy costume, so this is totally intentional. To top it off, David bought me a large Diet Coke and a medium popcorn, no butter, which is exactly what I like to have. He bought himself Reese's Pieces (which I love but never buy, because everyone will think I'm an oinker) and made a point of offering me some.

I feel like there's a massive conspiracy going on around me. Massive. It's not normal to have everything fall into place so perfectly. We laughed our asses off at dinner, talking about all kinds of things over TGI Friday's buffalo wings and Caesar salad—fun topics without a mention of Schwerinborg, my mother (I still assume that Jeremy and David do *not* know), or David's father's waaay conservative politics.

David brushed my hand a couple times under the table, and he even made the same jokes about the ketchup I always make. He kept grinning at me with his perfect mouth and his perfect eyes, both of which sparkled. (Okay, that might have been the

TGI Friday's lighting, but they sure seemed to have a sparkly kind of shine whenever he looked at me.)

It was *all* perfectly perfect, and anything that perfect makes me suspicious.

Especially since I am feeling WAY guilty now. To take my mind off the fact my evening—let alone my *life*—had been planned without my consent, I spent this afternoon going through all my e-mail from Vienna West, since I discovered that the high school didn't close my account like they were supposed to when I transferred to Schwerinborg.

And there it was. It almost made me call Christie and back out of the date-that's-not-officially-a-date.

COMMUNICATION. Actual communication from Georg.

His e-mail was dated yesterday, the day he got to Zermatt, and it said everything I've wanted to hear from him ever since the whole tabloid-newspaper-spin-control mess started.

He wants me. For real.

I know because that's what he told me the night of the dinner. We had that same aura of everything-tonight-is-perfect around us that's now being created between me and David in the movie theater. But that time, it didn't feel like a conspiracy. It just *happened*.

I shouldn't have come. Even before Mrs. Toleski showed up in her minivan to drive me (well, all of us) to TGI Friday's, I *knew* things would be okay with me and Georg. But then I figured nothing bad could happen if I just went along with Christie's plan and played it cool. David couldn't really be *that* interested in me. Half the girls in school would kill to go out with him, and I'm headed back to Schwerinborg in a week. And by not canceling, I keep Jules, Natalie, and especially Christie from giving me any more crap about it.

But now I'm feeling the vibe. The aura. The psychic whatever-it-is that makes me think this thing between me and David actually might be a *thing*.

Just like I felt with Georg.

I think.

They can't BOTH be true, can they? I can't possibly have feelings like this—that a relationship is cosmically ordained—for two completely different guys at the same time. It's just wrong, at least with one relationship, and maybe with both.

"You know that's completely inaccurate historically," David leans over and whispers in my ear as Heath strolls down a street that looks vaguely European and knocks on a weathered door.

I glance at David and smile, because I like that he's so smart and that he assumes I'm smart, too, since he's not bothering to point out what the on-screen inaccuracy is. "They didn't wear those until the late eighteen hundreds, at least," I whisper back, trying not to think about how solid David's shoulder feels where he's leaning it against mine. Must be all that rugby he plays. "No way would they have 'em in the Middle Ages, anyway."

"Bet Mrs. Bennett wouldn't have caught it," he says, close to my ear, and I try not to laugh aloud since we're smack in the middle of the movie and everyone in the theater's hush-hush.

We both turn our attention back to the screen, because the movie's really good (despite the costume inaccuracy), and a few seconds later he reaches across the armrest and puts his hand over mine. He's a little tentative (can he tell I'm totally freaking out?), but after a few seconds he laces his fingers through mine. He does it loosely so I can still pull away without being obvious.

But I don't. His fingers are long and warm and strong, and feel fabulous in between mine.

Most of my friends look at a guy's eyes, or at his shoulders and arms. With Jules, it's the way a guy's rear fits just so in his jeans. Me? I like a guy's hands, and I've always thought David's were the best. Well, except for Georg's. Maybe.

David doesn't look at me, but when I glance over at him he seems totally comfortable, like this is the normal course of events. I try to focus on Heath and the guy he's arguing with in the movie, but I've lost track of what's going on.

All I can think about is David. And Georg. I mean, doesn't David know there might be a thing between me and Georg? Is he kidding himself by holding my hand? Everyone else saw the newspaper, so I *know* he must've. He reads it every single day, first, because he's a natural news junkie, and second, because his dad's in it all the time. (All part of being a powerful Republican lobbyist, Dad once told me when I showed him an article about David's dad.)

And who am *I* kidding? There IS a thing between me and Georg, and if I hadn't been so crazy about the whole "cool it" phone call and had just freaking *asked* him to clarify things (even though, at the time, given the way our conversation went, I thought it would have sounded bizarre to ask him twice), I wouldn't be here. Feeling guilty.

Oh. My. God.

I am *cheating*.

Is this how Mom felt? Totally ripped up inside? Guilty? Or did she even care?

Because even though I know I love Georg, I'm feeling a total pull toward David. A *normal* girl wouldn't drool over a guy like I've drooled over David, then decide to yank her hand away when he finally holds it, would she?

Or when he tightens his fingers around hers, the way David's doing now? Because it feels really, REALLY good.

Maybe it's just that I'm not a normal girl.

"I'm glad you're home," he leans over and whispers. "I missed you, Winslow."

"Thanks—"

And then I feel it. Just the softest, most romantic kiss, right next to my ear. And I have no idea if this is a good thing—the thing I've wanted forever and can now get—or if it's the worst thing possible.

Seven

I am *so* glad we're in the back row of the theater and no one can see us without turning around and being obvious. With my luck, a reporter flew over from Schwerinborg and followed me into the Heath flick so he could snap a few more pictures. Or worse, maybe there's a private eye lurking in here. Someone hired by Steffi, because that's just the sort of thing nasty girls on soap operas always do when they want to get back at the nice girls. They make it their life's mission to prove the nice girls aren't so nice.

Steffi watches soaps. Lots of them. I think imitating soap opera bitches is how she became the evil demon spawn that she is.

Okay, I know my mind is going from highly unlikely possibilities (reporter) to downright whacked possibilities (Steffi), but given what's happened to me in the last few months, and what's happening *right now* . . .

I turn to give David a friendly warning look to discourage further kissing, since even though I like it, it's WRONG, but before I can get a word out, he leans in, his lips meet mine, and he's kissing me. This time, for real.

So I kiss him back.

Really, what can I do? I mean, he's RIGHT THERE. And the kissing's not bad.

In fact, it's actually pretty good. Deliberate and kind of daring, since Christie and Jeremy are sitting on my other side, plus who knows who else might get up to go pee and see us, since this theater's the closest one to Vienna West High School. But it's obvious from the way David's kissing me that he doesn't intend to have one of those grope-heavy sessions you always see other teenagers engaging in during the movies. Thankyou, thankyou, thankyou, David has more taste and class than that.

I guess, since his father's a semi-public figure, he's learned the tabloid lesson too.

But as his hand squeezes mine tighter for a split second (making me all warm and gooey inside), I can't help but wonder, *is this really okay?*

Of course, I've dreamed of kissing him FOREVER. I've had it so bad for him, I've even pretended that my pillow was David. (I did NOT kiss my pillow—*puh-leeze*—but I did go to sleep at night many, many times imagining I was putting my head on David's shoulder instead of a bunch of Poly-fil with a flannel cover.)

So I know if I could turn off my brain and forget that I theoretically have a boyfriend waiting for me a few thousand miles away, I would enjoy this immensely. David definitely knows what he's doing, though it's not as if I have much basis for comparison. Not even Christie suspects that Georg is the only guy I've ever kissed (well, besides Jason Barrows, which DOES NOT count).

It's totally pathetic, since I know people who are sleeping together, but there you go. I fake experience well, I guess.

David eases back and says in a voice barely loud enough for me to hear, "I've wanted to do that for a long time."

Not nearly as long as I have, but whatever. Hearing him say it makes all those years of lusting after him soooo worth it.

If he really means it.

Careful to play it cool, I just give him a little smile before turning my focus back to Heath (and trying to figure out what's going on in the movie, since now I'm completely lost).

A little over an hour later, we're in the back of Christie's mom's minivan. (I cannot WAIT until one of us can drive and Mrs. Toleski doesn't have to accompany us on every single evening out.) David and I are in the back seat, while Christie and Jeremy are in the middle, behind Christie's mom.

David let go of my hand right at the end of the movie so it wouldn't be obvious to Christie and Jeremy what was going on (even though I think Christie was probably trying to watch me out the corner of her eye as much as she was trying to watch the movie). But now, while Christie is telling her mom about what we had for dinner and Jeremy is picking something off the bottom of his shoe, David's making it clear he really is serious about this. He reaches his foot under the seat in front of us and hooks mine, where no one else can see, then gives me this very cute, slightly devious smile that makes my insides do a little dance of joy.

"You like the movie, Val?" he asks loud enough for everyone to hear.

"Sure—what wasn't to like?"

He shifts so he's slightly closer to me on the seat, and I realize what he was *really* asking me with that question. Geez, but I'm a dork.

"Which way is it again, Valerie?" Christie's mom asks, looking at me over her shoulder just before turning into the apartment complex where my mom and Gabby have their place. "I think I came in from the other direction when I picked you up."

"Take your first right—by the stop sign—then it's the second building on your right. Middle stairwell."

As she pulls into an empty parking spot along the curb in front of Mom's building, David asks, "Want me to walk you to the door?"

The sidewalk from the street to the stairwell door is about a hundred feet long, but I'm perfectly capable of walking by myself, even though it's midnight. I mean, we're in a nice part of town, and Mrs. Toleski can see all the way from the van to the front door—it's no dark alley or anything.

"I'm fine," I say as Christie and Jeremy scoot over so I can climb past the middle row of seats and out the sliding door.

"I'd feel better if David walked you up," Mrs. Toleski says, which I suspected she would (she's cautious—probably comes from having been a nun), so David hops out of the van behind me before I can argue.

Secretly, though, I'm kind of glad he's with me. Not because I think there's a wacko lurking in the bushes, though. Just because.

I thank Mrs. Toleski, say bye to Jeremy and Christie (while trying to ignore the self-satisfied grin on Christie's face), and turn toward the apartment, with David right off my elbow. I can tell from the way he's walking, close to me but with his hands very carefully tucked into his front pockets, that he's hyper-aware of our proximity and the fact we're on a mostly dark sidewalk with all the stars out overhead. The clear skies and the soft breeze around us make the atmosphere totally romantic in a way you usually only see on sappy TV movies.

I've always known when David was within a shouting distance of me—I've developed a well-honed radar regarding the guy—but this is the first time I've been positive *he's* really noticing *me*.

And it's pretty cool.

We step up onto the wide stair outside the heavy glass door leading to my mom's new apartment and I fish around in my purse for the key Mom gave me—mostly so I don't have to stand there feeling awkward, wondering if he's going to kiss me good night.

"Must be hard seeing your mom living in an apartment all by herself," he says. "I couldn't imagine having to deal with a divorce or trying to choose between parents."

"Yeah," I say. He clearly doesn't know the whole story, which means Christie has kept her word—so far. I'm tempted to tell David the truth about my parents, even though we only have a minute. First, I want to be certain he hears it from me instead of from gossip central, and second, I'm curious about how he'll react. But I keep my mouth shut. Just for tonight, I don't want to know.

He bites his bottom lip, which I've never seen him do. David Anderson isn't the nervous type.

"What's wrong?"

He shrugs. "I just wish you weren't going back to Europe, I guess. That you'd consider staying here with your mom. I know living in the apartment means you'd have to go to school at Lake Braddock instead of Vienna West, but it'd make Christie real happy. She's been moping around like you wouldn't believe since you left." He hesitates for a second before adding, "It'd make me happy too."

Whoa. If it was possible for a person to make one wish and have it come true, this is what I would have wished for. But why-oh-why-why-why couldn't he have said this to me a year ago? Or on any day at all since, oh, KINDERGARTEN? I was just getting over him, coming to terms with the fact I'm his Armor Girl, and that being the Armor Girl isn't such a bad thing.

Does he not realize what he is doing to me here?

"They're watching us," I say, rolling my eyes in the direction of the curb. Part of me wants him to kiss me, *now,* but common sense (and the fact I can see Christie staring at me through the side window of the minivan) tells me that this is sooo not the time.

"I know. Otherwise, I wouldn't be standing here with my hands in my pockets. They'd be somewhere else."

Okay, now I think I'm going to die. Right here on the front step of a suburban, ugly-ass apartment building.

And I'd die a happy girl.

As I slide the key into the lock, he takes a step down so he's on the sidewalk leading back to Mrs. Toleski's van. "Maybe we can get together tomorrow night? I can ask my brother to drive us somewhere. I know it's lame, but I bet he'd—"

"Can I e-mail you tomorrow?" I need time to clear my head.

"You have my address?"

I nod. He gave it to me a few days before I left for Schwerinborg and asked me to keep in touch, but I never wrote. It didn't feel right, since I'd never e-mailed or IM'ed with him while I was living here.

But that doesn't mean I didn't memorize his e-addy the second he gave it to me.

"Before you go back, I think we should at least talk."

I swallow hard. Wow, but I can tell from his face that he really means what he's saying, and it's making me insane because if I stand here one second longer, I'll grab him and kiss him first. Christie watching and all.

"I'll e-mail in the morning," I say, surprising myself with how calm I sound.

I turn the key and walk into the lobby as casually as I can. When I turn to take the stairs up to the third floor, where my mom's apartment is, I see David strolling toward the van. His hands are still in his front pockets, which makes his jeans pull across his rear just enough to make me take a good, long look.

Yee-ow.

I have no clue what I'm going to do.

"How was your night, honey?"

"You're still up?" My mom's never been a night owl—she usually goes to bed at nine thirty, sometimes ten if there's a good TV show on. But it's past eleven thirty now, and since she's sitting in an armchair with her reading lamp on and the rest of the apartment's dark, I figure she's up for one reason and one reason only.

Me.

"I wanted to get some time alone with you," Mom says with a smile. She sets down her book—I notice she's barely started it, which means she wasn't really reading—and reaches out to pat the arm of the chair next to hers. "Sit and tell me about it."

I leave my purse by the door, then drop into the empty chair. "The movie was great. Wasn't your style, though. Very commercial and big budget." My mom loves indie flicks—all the stuff they show at festivals—that usually have choppy editing and too-deep-for-normal-people-to-understand hidden meaning. Dad and I always used to tease her about it. Most years, she hasn't seen any of the Best Picture nominees for the Oscar.

"Was it the historical film with Heath Ledger?"

Historical film? She's making it sound like it should be on A&E. I keep a straight face and reply, "Well, you know I wouldn't miss Heath."

"Bet he looked pretty hot, too."

Come again? She's mocked my Heath obsession forever, but I have to wonder, does SHE actually think he looks good? And then I totally crack up, because I can see from her face that she said it to be funny.

"You looked like you could use a good laugh," she says.

"Definitely."

I know, I know. It's a strange thing to bond over, but I'm gonna take what I can get.

"Gabrielle's asleep already. I thought it might be a good time for the two of us to just sit and chat—if you're not too tired."

"Sure." I'm beat, even though I took a nap after the girls left this afternoon just so I wouldn't crash at the movie, but I figure now's as good a time as any to talk to her—especially if she's in a jokey mood.

She looks a little uncomfortable even though she's still smiling, and I get the impression she wants to talk about Dad—how he's getting along in Schwerinborg, if he's seeing anyone, if he's making sure I'm eating healthy food, all that kind of thing.

Since the absolute last thing I want to do is report to Mom about Dad, or vice versa (mostly because Jules warned me about this happening and says not to even think about telling one parent about the other), I decide to make a pre-emptive strike. "You know, this afternoon I saw you kiss Gabrielle on the cheek in the kitchen when I was talking with the girls."

One of Mom's eyebrows arches up at this, but I keep going. "I know you two are trying to keep things low-key so you won't freak me out. I mean, it was obvious at the airport. You never got within arm's reach of her, but you kept giving each other looks when you thought I wasn't watching."

"Was that upsetting to you?"

"No. Not really." I pick at a piece of lint on the arm of the chair, then make a face. "Well, maybe it was. But I think you two should just act normal around me, even if I'm only here for a week. Dad says we'll move back here for good after the next election, no matter who wins the White House, so I'm going to have to get used to you guys being together sooner or later."

Mom reaches over and puts her hand on top of mine. "Gabby and I are doing our best to make this transition as painless as possible for you."

"I know that."

"But you're still pretty uncomfortable with it?"

I nod. "I don't have a problem with you being gay, I don't think. It's more that you found someone else so fast. I mean, even if you'd hooked up with a guy, I'd be torqued by all of this."

Mom is quiet, and I know she wants me

to look at her. When I do, she just tilts her head and gives me one of those looks that says she knows better.

"Fine, I'm uncomfortable with the gay thing too. But I'm trying very hard not to be. I don't *want* to be."

"I appreciate that. More than you can ever know." She gives my hand a squeeze and her eyes get all watery. "It might not seem like it sometimes, but you're the most important person in my whole life, Valerie. I'd do anything for you and I want you to know that."

"I do."

"But I can't not be who I am."

In a completely non-snarky voice, I say, "You made that very clear."

"I never wanted to hurt you or your father. I love him very much, and I always will. But when I met Gabrielle, I realized why I've been so . . . well, that's probably a whole different conversation. Suffice it to say I realized that I'd been living a lie, and I finally understood, deep in my soul, why my marriage to your father never felt quite right. It wasn't easy for me to do what I did, and it took me a long time to work up the courage to leave. Mostly because I was afraid of how it'd affect you and your father. I didn't want you to be hurt."

"It did hurt, though." It *still* hurts. "But I know it wasn't on purpose. And Dad's been great about it all. He's never said one bad thing about you."

"Well, that's something, I suppose." She wipes her eyes with the back of her hand and stands up. "I think we woke up Gabrielle."

At that moment, I hear the toilet in the hall bathroom flush. "Sorry. I was probably talking too loud. She won't be pissed, will she?"

"Don't say 'pissed'—your father will kill me if you go back to Schwerinborg using that kind of language," she says, though she's smiling. "And no, she won't be."

A minute later, Gabrielle comes out into the living room. She has a sleepy look on her face and her hair's looking pretty bad, but she seems agreeable enough, so I doubt she overheard anything. Not that she isn't already aware of everything we talked about, anyway.

"How was your date, Valerie?"

I give her the Valerie Shrug. "Okay, I guess." Like I'm going to discuss my love life with Gabrielle when I can barely talk about it with my parents—though I do give her props for being courteous enough to ask.

"Your friends seem pretty cool. I really like Christie. Jeremy and David are nice, too."

Damn straight. "Thanks, I've always thought so."

Mom gives my shoulder a quick squeeze—probably for being polite to Gabby—then starts organizing the magazines on the coffee table, which is always the signal she's about to go to bed. "Gabrielle and I wanted to take you someplace tomorrow as a surprise, but I just had another thought. If I can get appointments, how about if we go to that day spa we always liked in Vienna first?"

"That'd be cool." I haven't had a manicure in ages and ages, and I love getting them. Maybe, if Mom's feeling particularly guilty and they have an opening, I can get a facial, too. That'd rock.

But then I see a little look pass between

Gabrielle and my mom. I get the feeling that wherever else they were—or are—planning to take me isn't going to be something I'll like.

"So what's the surprise?"

Mom gives me a grin that's way too perky for this time of night. "Just that. A surprise. But I promise, you'll like it."

Right.

"What do you think?" I lean forward, pulling the seat belt to its max so I can extend my fingers into the gap between the two front seats of Mom's SUV to show off my manicure.

"Love that red!" Gabrielle says, inspecting my nails. "What shade was that? I must've missed it."

"It's called Rock the Vote Red. It's one of the Nicole colors." I usually go for pinks, but the name of the polish screamed out to me. I figured picking "Rock the Vote" would be a good luck charm to make doubly sure whoever wins the White House in November hires (or remembers to rehire, in President Carew's case) my dad.

I can only hope.

"Very pretty," my mom says. "Which did you end up with, Gabby?"

"OPI British collection. Blushingham Palace." She waggles her pink-tipped fingers in the air, and her whole attitude reminds me that she's a freaking DECADE younger than my mom—at least. "I think I like your Rock the Vote color better, though. I'm going to have to remember to look at the Nicole colors next time we go back. I love supporting them, since the company gives so much money to charitable causes."

Of course.

"I bought a bottle so I could do touch-ups," I tell her. "I'm probably not going to take it on the plane, so you can have it if you want."

"Are you sure?"

"Sure." The more people who wear get-Dad-his-job-back polish the better. Plus, for my mom's sake, I figure I'm going to have to be nice to Gabrielle eventually. She might be a mom-stealer, and she might've made me eat whole-grain pancakes for breakfast (made with soy milk, which gave them a bizarre aftertaste—and pancakes should *not* have an aftertaste), but maybe, if I try reeeeally hard, I can convince myself she's not so bad.

I see Mom smile to herself. "Maybe I'll try out the color, then, too."

"I've never seen you use color." I look at Gabrielle. "Really. She's worn nude polish or had a French manicure for as long as I can remember. Red would be a serious departure for her."

"Well, life's an adventure. We'll drag your mother along kicking and screaming if we have to, right Valerie?" She reaches back to rub my head, like I'm in kindergarten or something. "She needs a little change in her life!"

Okay. Bonding moment over. The whole life's-an-adventure philosophy is too much like that moving cheese book's philosophy (yeah, I flipped through it, so sue me) and I do *not* need to be reminded of the cheese book.

"So will you tell me where we're going now?" We're headed out of Vienna, toward Burke. "Or is it still a surprise?"

"Hang on for another five minutes, honey, and we'll be there." She's still smiling, but the smile's not reaching her eyes anymore. Wherever we're going, I can tell she's worried I might not like it.

And if she thinks that, I can safely assume I won't.

Mom turns the SUV onto a suburban street, taking us through a neighborhood of colonial and Tudor-style homes, all with yards kept pristine by landscaping services. We pass a neighborhood park, then she slows down as we approach a church. Apprehension gets the better of me as we pull into the parking lot. There are six or seven cars parked by the back door, and that's where Mom pulls in too.

"Um, Mom? You're Episcopalian." And I'm guessing Gabrielle believes only in Evangelical Vegetarianism. "You might've deduced from the red flag draped over the cross and the big sign out front that this is a Methodist establishment. And it isn't even Sunday."

"I'm well aware of the date and our location."

"Are we going to a Bible study?" A gay Bible study, maybe? If so, this would take the cake. And it's the kind of thing I can totally see Mom wanting to bring me to, hoping it'll make me feel better about her and Gabrielle, and to keep me from believing the Religious Right types who are bound to tell me that Mom and Gabby are going to hell, or that what they're doing makes them not good Christians anymore.

We always went to church together—me, Mom, and Dad—until Mom moved out. Dad only goes sporadically in Schwerinborg, and I've gone with him, but I figure Mom's been going all along. And she definitely believes in God, so I know she's not going to hell.

But a Methodist church? Are they more open to gays or something? I know there were a few articles in the newspaper a while back about some gay pastor (or bishop?) in New Hampshire, but I can't remember what kind of church it was.

Or if it was even New Hampshire. Could have been Vermont.

"It's not a Bible study." Mom shuts off the ignition and gestures for me to unbuckle 'cause she apparently wants me to come into the church. As she opens the back door for me, she says, "It's a pee-flag support group meeting."

As I follow Mom and Gabrielle across the parking lot, I shoot her a look that says, *support group*? And *Pee Flag*? "A what?"

"P-F-L-A-G. Parents, Families and Friends of Lesbians and Gays."

"We thought you'd enjoy sitting in on a meeting while you're home," Gabrielle adds, pushing open the back door and leading us down a semidark hallway. I'm getting a real queasy feeling, and she must be able to tell, because she looks over her shoulder and adds, "You don't have to participate, just listen. I think, if you allow your heart and mind to stay open to the discussion, you'll come to understand that you're not alone in your world experience. That your mother is better for coming out, and that you'll be better for it, too, in the long run."

I'm so not wanting to hear Gabby's psychobabble. As if my mind needs more opening to world experience. I mean, what does she think I got being shipped off to live in *Schwerinborg*?!

And BETTER FOR IT? How in the

world did she say that with a straight face?!

I put my hand on Mom's elbow to attempt a last-minute appeal. "Can't we—"

"Don't worry, it'll be fine." Mom opens the door to a brightly lit room with about a dozen people mingling inside and drinking coffee from a big silver urn. A guy who I'd put at about seventeen years old waves to Mom. She gives me a little push into the room, then introduces me to "John" before I can even argue. "I'm sure you two will have a lot to talk about," she says.

I mumble something vaguely polite to John, because Dad has drilled *polite* into my head from birth, but I can't focus on John at all. I'm still trying to process Pee-Flag and the fact I'm here and simply *do not* belong. I mean, PLEASE. My mom has definitely flipped out this time.

This is way worse than a self-help book.

"Hi, Valerie!" one of the women says as she bounces—and I do mean bounces—across the room to stand beside John Boy. Her smile is totally Joan Rivers fake—as in I'm wondering if it's been surgically uplifted—and it's clear she knows Mom (and who I am) and that this whole

PFLAG ambush has been planned.

"Great, you're here!" Mom says to Bouncy Lady. "I'll be back in an hour for Valerie—I know she's in good hands."

"You're leaving?" I hiss, trying not to be rude but really not caring at this point. How can she LEAVE ME here?

But she and Gabrielle scoot out the door without even bothering to answer me, and I'm stuck all alone in a room full of strange people. Worse, every last one of them is staring at me like I'm the newest attraction in the National Zoo's primate exhibit.

Great.

I glance toward a wooden rack on the rear wall of the room. It's filled with brochures about the church. I focus on one with a little cross on the front, mostly so I don't have to look at Bouncy Lady and John Boy and let them see my panic.

God, get me through this, please, I scream inside my head.

Because if I don't end up on some psychiatrist's couch soon, it truly will be an act of God.

Eight

"I'm Yolanda. I'm the group leader," Bouncy Lady says. I wonder if she's on uppers or something, but decide that no, she's just one of those fidgety people who hops around like a little kid her entire life. Like she's on a permanent Kool-Aid rush.

"Hi, Yolanda. Nice to meet you." I shake her hand, but I feel like a complete idiot. A *trapped* idiot. I tilt my head toward a bunch of gray metal folding chairs, which are arranged in a C-shape in three rows at the other end of the room. A couple of people are sitting there with their coffee, but most of the chairs are empty while everyone stands and yaks in little groups. "Um, should I just sit?"

"Sure, make yourself comfortable. We'll be starting our meeting in just a minute. There's coffee and soda, if you'd like a drink."

I tell her thanks, I'll grab a Diet Coke (because I need one, bad), but then she gets all squealy as someone else—a woman about my mom's age—walks through the door.

It's the freaking Twilight Zone in here.

John pops the top on a Diet Coke and hands it to me. In a hushed voice he says, "Yolanda's always like that. The rest of us are much closer to normal."

I take the drink and give him a grateful smile.

"Your mom just dumped you here without warning you, didn't she?"

"It's that obvious, huh?" I can't help but like the guy. I get the impression he's being genuinely nice—that he hasn't been coached to say this stuff just to make me comfortable.

He shoves his hair out of his face. It's scruffy brown and too long to be stylish, and he's wearing a Kenny Chesney T-shirt. He's not bad looking—he's got a killer bod and a decent enough face—but he's definitely not the kind of guy who hangs with the "in" crowd.

Which, of course, means he probably realizes I'm not exactly cool either.

"My parents brought me without telling me what it was all about the first time either," he explains. "My mom's not here today, but she still comes sometimes."

How do I ask this? "So, is your dad, um—"

"No. My older brother, Brad. He came out last year."

"Oh." I can't imagine a buffed-up, grungy guy like John with a gay brother— let alone a gay brother named Brad, which sounds like a pretty non-gay name. He just doesn't look the type.

Then again, what's the type? Do I look like the daughter of a lesbian?

I take a long sip of my Diet Coke, telling myself that I must be way more shallow than I thought for making such an asinine snap judgment about John. Or for making judgments like that about anyone.

"The group's not so bad," he says, keeping his voice low. "The first time I came, I was pissed off like you wouldn't believe. Couldn't believe my parents were dragging me to something like this. So I know where you're coming from."

"And you're here by choice now?"

One side of his mouth crooks into a smile. "Yeah, believe it or not. I don't come to all the meetings, but most of 'em. I'm going to NYU next year, and between making college plans and everything that's been going on with my brother, I'm completely stressed out. This helps me keep my head on straight." He pauses for a sec, then adds, "So to speak."

Did he just make a gay joke? In a room full of people who've got to be sensitive to the issue?

"I was planning to share an apartment with Brad in New York, since he's already at NYU, but now I'm not sure, you know? I mean, what if he gets a boyfriend or something?"

"Yeah, I can understand that." That would suck way worse than my situation.

Yolanda starts herding everyone toward

the folding chairs, so I quickly grab a seat as far back as possible. It's a small room, though, and with only a dozen people in it, I can't really hide out.

Especially since Yolanda is now POINTING AT ME. "We have a new member today." Her voice reminds me of a varsity cheerleader. Or worse, a wannabe varsity cheerleader. "Everyone please welcome Valerie!"

There's a murmur of hellos, then Yolanda says, "Valerie, why don't you tell us why you're here today?"

"Ummmm . . ." Because my mother TRICKED ME? And what about Gabrielle telling me I didn't have to talk if I didn't want to? I want to give Yolanda the Valerie Shrug, but every single person is staring at me.

I'm going to KILL my mother.

"I guess I'm just here to listen," I finally say.

Thankfully, Yolanda seems to accept this, and moves on to talk about her week. Apparently, her daughter, Amy, is gay. Sounds like they get along well enough, but Yolanda's worried about Amy moving into a new apartment complex—and that Amy's older, more conservative neighbors will treat her differently or will say nasty things when they discover she's not coming with a nice young husband, 2.5 kids, and a minivan.

"Amy doesn't seem too concerned, though," Yolanda tells the group. "She admits that the neighbors will probably react badly, but she doesn't think they'll pay enough attention to her to figure it out right away. So I'm just trying to trust in Amy, and trying not to worry."

A few people offer encouragement, which makes Yolanda smile. "So, anyone else with something to share? Anything happen in the last two weeks?"

She points to a guy in the front row with his arms crossed over his chest who's raising a finger in the air. Not a hand, just a finger. He says his name is Mel (for my benefit, I'm sure, though I can guarantee I won't remember his name five minutes from now). Mel, a balding guy with a beer gut and tattoos on his knuckles, talks about meeting his son's new partner for the first time last weekend. How he felt strange seeing his son kiss another man, even though there wasn't full-on tongue action or anything.

"Caught me completely off-guard, I'll tell ya. I guess I should've seen it comin', though," he says with a sarcastic laugh. "Ever since Jake was little, I figgered the day'd come where he'd call and tell us he met a young lady—someone from college or from his fancy office—and that he wanted to get married and give me and my wife a bunch of grandchildren."

Mel scratches his chin for a minute, then adds, "I've adjusted to the fact he ain't never gonna have a wife. But seeing him kiss another man just—" He stops for a second and closes his eyes. When he opens them again, he says, "I guess it just hit home all over again that everything I pictured for my boy ain't gonna come to pass. I drove home from the restaurant mad. Real mad."

I start thinking about Mom kissing Gabrielle, and I can totally identify with this guy. Even if he is, like, sixty or so. And I'm willing to bet he has anger issues regardless of his son's sexual orientation, if his deep frown lines and rough voice are anything to go by.

"Did the kiss make you question your love for your son?" A woman sitting in the front row, on the opposite side of the C-shape from Mel, asks.

Mel thinks about it for a moment. "I don't think so. I love the kid, no matter what. But I sure was angry. I wanted to take a swing at his . . . his *partner* . . . just knock the fag's head off. Never would, course. I know in my gut that this is all *my* problem—not Jake's, and not his partner's. But ya know, people just didn't *do* this sort of thing where I was raised. Ya went to school, worked hard, and got married. Period. I guess what I'm saying is, I still have days where I feel like Jake's intentionally trying to ruin *my* life. So that's why I came this week, even though I ain't been here in a couple months. To try not to be so damned angry."

To my left, I hear John clear his throat. "I was really ripshit a few months ago— you know, wondering if I was going to have a place to live after I made all these plans. I wanted to call up my brother in New York and just tell him off."

Wow. I wouldn't use the word "ripshit" in this crowd—let alone that we're in the basement of a *church*—but no one even blinks when John talks this way. As I look around and listen to the people whispering, I realize they all pretty much talk however they want to, and all seem to accept how everyone else talks. Even Mel calling his son's partner a fag, which is another word I'd never use around this crowd.

Not that I'm going to actually *talk*. But it is interesting.

"Anyway," John says, "I read somewhere that a good exercise is to put all the things that bother you about a person down one side of a paper, and all the things you love down the other side. So I made myself do that before I picked up the phone."

Like a pro and con list? someone asks.

He nods. "It sounds stupid, because you sort of know it all in your head already, but when I listed everything out on paper, I could see exactly what was bothering me about my brother, in black and white."

"And it helped you deal with those issues?" Yolanda asks.

"Exactly. And it's been good having a concrete list of things I love about my brother, 'cause I can read it whenever I need to remind myself to chill out."

He leans forward in his chair and pushes his hair off his face again. "Having a gay brother is really small stuff when I think about it. I mean, I'd choose having him tell me he's gay over telling me he has cancer any day. Like Mel said, it reminds me that I'm the one with a problem, not him. It's just part of who he is."

John's use of the phrase "small stuff" reminds me of the self-help book Mom sent to me in Schwerinborg a few weeks ago, and of course, that reminds me of the ridiculous cheese book. The one that said I have to anticipate change in the same way I'm supposed to anticipate that the cheese in the fridge will go bad, and go out and get new cheese. Or something.

But now that John's talking, I'm thinking that even though the cheese book sounded pretty bizarre, the small stuff book was kind of useful. Maybe I should give John's list idea a chance too.

I'm not one for exercises. I mean, I hate taking those quizzes in teen magazines that are supposed to tell me what kind of guy would be perfect for me, what kind of clothes fit my personality, or all about my dosha. But this exercise seems to make sense, because as John tells the group about what he wrote on his lists, I find that I'm mentally making lists for Mom. When I can't keep track anymore, I pick up a Methodist church flyer that's lying on the floor under the chair in front of me and scribble, keeping the print super-small so no one else can read it.

The Cons:
- *Gabrielle (I think. Jury's still out.)*
- *Probably lied to me (about being gay, about cheating)*
- *Put Dad through hell, and he did NOT deserve it*
- *Explaining everything to my friends blows*
- *Sends self-help books in (misguided) attempt to make me happy*

The Pros:

- *She loves me.*
- *Didn't mean to lie to me (or lied for the right reasons?)*
- *Brought me here, and I never would have come on my own (Possibly a con? Probably a pro, since I'm making this list.)*
- *Trying to be open with me now*
- *Trying to treat me like an adult (with exception of today's kidnapping)*
- *Told me I could choose where to live, with her or with Dad (understanding that the choice should be MINE)*
- *Cool to my friends*
- *Took me for manicure (though as a possible setup)*
- *Tried to make marriage work for years so she wouldn't hurt me or Dad*

As I keep scribbling to the bottom of the page, I realize that while the cons on my list are biggies, they all have to do with me and my attitude.

Okay, I'm not happy that my parents don't live together anymore. I can add that to the cons list. But otherwise, like John discovered when he made his lists, most of the cons have to do with *me* being angry or uncomfortable or disappointed.

The pros, on the other hand, have to do with my mother herself: that she loves me, and that she never would have come out if she hadn't felt like she absolutely had to. The pros are all things that won't change. And five years from now, the cons look like things that MIGHT not matter so much.

Well, maybe not the cheating.

Maybe I need to just suck it up, deal, and grow up a little. Though apparently (judging from Mel and the rest of the room), it's one of those things that's easier said than done.

I'm egotistical enough to think I have better emotional management skills than Mel, though. And if John can learn to deal—or at least try to deal—maybe I can too.

"How was it, honey?"

"Not as bad as I thought," I admit as I climb into the back of Mom's Toyota. I never did talk, but at the end of the meeting, I did check out the table of books Yolanda had on display. Some weren't for me, like *Our Trans Children* (sheesh, I REALLY hope I never need that one, though I did see one woman pick it up and she looked relieved to have found it), but there was one called *Is Homosexuality a Sin?*

I grabbed that one.

Before I went outside to meet my mother, though, I hid it under my shirt. Totally immature, but I don't care. I don't want her to know I'm worried about this.

I mean, I'm *not*. I don't think she's committing a sin against God. I figure He wired her the way He did for a reason. But I still want to read the book. I have a feeling other people *do* think Mom is living a sinful life, and sooner or later, they're going to tell me so. Some may just be concerned, like Christie (and maybe Christie's mom—I don't know). But what about the serious gay-bashers? The kind of people Yolanda was worried might harass her daughter when she moved into a new apartment, maybe egging her house or yelling at her to repent? I have no idea how to handle that kind of thing.

Mom puts her key in the ignition, but before she starts the engine, I lean forward into the front seat, totally ignoring Gabrielle, and give my mother my toughest stare. "But don't ever, ever spring something like that on me again. I mean it, Mom."

I know I shouldn't talk to her this way, but I have to get it through her head—and Gabrielle's—that leaving me at the PFLAG meeting without telling me what I was about to face was totally uncool.

"I know we probably could've handled it better," Mom says with a big sigh. "We've talked about it ever since we heard from your father that you were coming to visit. And we talked about it the whole time we were waiting for you."

"You waited outside?"

"Down the street." Gabrielle has the good sense to look embarrassed. "Your mom and I didn't want you to see us out the window and come running back to the car."

"Very mature of you both." Freaks. I'm in a Toyota SUV with freaks.

"I'm really sorry, honey," Mom says,

sounding mostly sincere. "But I knew you'd never go otherwise, and I wanted you to try it out at least once just so you'd hear what other people in your situation are doing to deal with their concerns, and to see that you have resources."

"Yeah, I kind of got that."

"Well, I won't do it again. All right?"

I just give a little huff as I sit back in my seat and buckle my belt. I forgive her, but ONLY if she keeps her word and doesn't pull this crap again. Even if it *was* helpful.

She flicks her gaze toward me as she turns to back up the Toyota. "So was it helpful?"

Can she read my mind?

"I guess." Doesn't mean I'm all happy happy happy about her being a lesbian, but I do feel better than I did before I came to Virginia. Well, about the whole gay-mom thing. The who-the-hell-am-I-dating? issue is something else entirely. Coming home made that a lot worse.

"Well, when you come to visit me during your school break this summer, maybe you can go again. Just for reassurance, or if you have anything you need to talk about. I promise not to spring it on you if you do." Mom's face squinches into a grimace when I shoot her a death look. "Sorry. I'll drop the whole subject. I'm just glad you went and I hope you'll consider going again next time you come."

I shrug. Maybe.

"So," she says as she turns the SUV out of the parking lot and back toward the apartment, "what did you think of John? He seemed very nice."

"He's fine."

"Maybe if things with David don't work out, or with that boy in Schwerinborg . . ."

That *boy*?

"Mom, I soooo do not need you playing matchmaker for me. I have enough trouble with Christie, Jules, and Natalie as it is."

"All right, all right," Mom says. "But did you notice that he's a Kenny Chesney fan? I love Kenny Chesney."

"Mom? NO."

To: Val@viennawest.edu
From: BarbnGabby@mailmagic.com
Subject: FWD: FOR VALERIE

Valerie, this is from your father. Mom.

— — —

To: BarbnGabby@mailmagic.com
From: MartWins@realmail.sg.com
Subject: FOR VALERIE

Barb, I don't know if Val still has an e-mail account there, or if she can access her Schwerinborg e-mail from your apartment. Either way, would you please forward this to her at the proper address? Hope all is well. Martin

— — —

Dear Valerie,

Sorry I had to send this via your mother's e-mail account. I know you'll be back here in a few days, but I wanted to touch base with you before you return, and I'm usually working during the hours when you're home to take a phone call.

I've met with the press office, and things here look positive. They pinpointed the source of the leak. It seems one of your schoolmates overheard a conversation and told several friends. That student's father has the situation in hand and has dealt with it.

The only story that's been in the press since you left simply mentioned that you flew home for vacation. There has been no more speculation about anything questionable where you're concerned. The press about Prince Georg's trip to Zermatt and his charity stops at hospitals has all been positive.

So please, do not worry. And if you do keep in touch with your friends here, I think it best to not mention the incident. They understand that they were wrong to gossip in the school halls about these matters, and that what they believed happened at the palace was, in fact, not true.

I'll pick you up at the airport when you arrive. I'll meet you just outside the security gate.

It'll be good to have you home again. I want to hear all about your trip, and I have quite a bit to tell you, too.

Love, Dad.

To: RugbyDave@viennawest.edu
From: Val@viennawest.edu
Subject: Hi

Hi, David.

First, I must ask—RugbyDave? I know you play rugby, but I've never heard ANYONE call you Dave. Just David.

Second, if you're still interested, and if your brother is willing to drive, I can go out tonight. Have to be home by 11:30.

Valerie

To: Val@viennawest.edu
From: RugbyDave@viennawest.edu
Subject: Re: Hi

Hey, Valerie.

To answer your question—I definitely prefer David to Dave. My family calls me Dave, though, and I thought "RugbyDavid" sounded stupid. So there you go.

And yes. I'm still interested. Yes, my brother can take us out and pick us up in time to get you home. (I'll have my cell, so I can call him whenever.)

How about if I get you at 6:30? I remember how to get to your mom's place. We can go out to dinner near the mall, if you'd like, so we can walk over for a movie if we want afterward. Or do whatever.

See you tonight,
David-but-please-not-Dave

To: RugbyDave@viennawest.edu
From: Val@viennawest.edu
Subject: Re: Hi

6:30 is fine. I'll watch out the window and come down so you won't have to buzz. (Believe me, you're better off not coming inside—my mom will ask a zillion questions.)

And I promise not to call you Dave. You're definitely a David.

Later,
Valerie-who-IS-also-Val

To: Val@viennawest.edu
From: ChristieT@viennawest.edu
Subject: WHOO-HOOOOOOO!!!!

Valerie,

Did last night not ROCK? I saw you and David holding hands in the movies, and I THOUGHT I saw him kiss you. Did he? Does this mean you're going to give him a chance? (And does this all make you feel better about everything with your mom?)

Just a sec, Jeremy's on the phone. . . .

WHY ARE YOU NOT CALLING ME THIS SEC-OND?!? Jeremy says David just e-mailed him and said that the two of you are going out again tonight!

I KNEW IT!!! I am SO FREAKING THRILLED FOR YOU!!

I just knew this would work out. You two belong together. Jeremy says David sounds totally pumped about the whole thing too. (It's about time—this should have happened in jr. high, if you ask me!)

Anyway, call me FIRST THING tomorrow morning to let me know what happens, 'kay? I am DYING.

AND—I really hope this makes you feel better about everything that's going on with your mom. I'm here for you if you EVER need to talk about all that, okay? No judgments, no worries—got it?

Your extremely happy friend,
Christie

Nine

"Ladies and gentlemen, you're about to have your asses kicked by two sopho-mores."

I can't help but grin at David's remark as we huddle over a sticky round table in the bar area of TGI Friday's. We just ate here last night, but we figured it'd be easi-est to eat here again since it's next door to the movie theater. (Plus, I've had a serious jones for American French fries for a while now. They just aren't the same in Schwerinborg.)

In the end, though, we skipped the movies because, with the obvious exception of Heath's new flick, they all sucked. Plus,

TGI Friday's has a trivia game running on the television screens (well, on the TVs that aren't showing college basketball, which I don't give a rat's ass about), and tons of people are playing. This presented us the opportunity to do what the two of us do best and show off our geeky smartness—without Christie or Jeremy here to make fun of us—and we couldn't resist.

"You just *know* we're the only ones who'll get this," I say, carefully tapping the D key for *Badajoz* on the answer pad, because we both (naturally) knew that was where the British surrounded a French fortress in March 1812.

"I dunno." David studies the rows of restaurant booths on our right, then slides a look to our left, toward a married couple sitting at the bar with a trivia pad in front of them. "I think they're the ones who got that question about Henry the Eighth right."

We decided earlier—judging from their intense focus, expensive gray suits, and the briefcases they have tucked in front of their barstools—that they're lawyers or investment bankers or something else requiring a fair amount of smarts. And that they're probably our toughest competition.

"Yeah, I think so too. But this question is way more obscure. I wouldn't have known it if it hadn't been drilled into us in European History last year."

We watch the television as two of the wrong answers, the Falkland Islands (as if!) and Trier disappear from the screen, leaving Badajoz and Casablanca.

"Not many people know that Jane Seymour was Henry the Eighth's third wife, though," he argues, eyeing the couple at the bar. "They only know the Jane Seymour from television—as in Dr. Quinn, Medicine Woman. If they knew about the original Jane Seymour, they'll know Badajoz."

"No way. Remember how we learned about Henry's wives back in eighth grade?" I reel them off on my fingers, along with the little ditty our teacher taught us to help memorize what happened to each of them. "Divorced, beheaded, died, divorced, beheaded, survived. Every kid learns that one. And since only one wife died—well, other than from having her head lopped off—she's easier to remember."

"You get off on knowing this kind of useless information, don't you?"

His smile is so perfect, I have to smile back. "Yeah. And you do, too, so shut up."

David puts his hand over mine on the table. He gives it a subtle tug, urging me to look at the couple again, so I do—just in time to see them switch their answer. They must've had Trier.

The television flashes the correct answer: Badajoz. Then the scores pop up, and we were the only ones to get it right.

"Do we rock, or what?" He sounds totally shocked. "There's only one question left, and unless we completely blow it, they can't catch us."

The couple at the bar look around, scanning the rest of the people sitting at the bar with drinks and trivia pads, then past us to analyze the players at dinner tables.

"They can't figure out who knew it," David says. "They assume it's one of the other groups of adults. Or someone who made a lucky guess."

"You'd think they'd know better." I

look up at the scores, which are still flash-
ing. David put our team name in the trivia
pad as V.D.—totally juvenile, but also
kind of funny, since it's hysterical hearing
other teams speculate about the identity of
V.D. And whether V.D. actually has V.D.

We get the last question right—what
does a milliner make? (hats)—but so do a
lot of other people. Doesn't matter, though,
because we just beat at least ten other
teams.

"I feel like such a geek," I tell him.

"You've got a pocket protector I don't
know about?"

"No."

"You sit at home trying to come up
with new scientific theories, just for fun?"

"Definitely not."

He scoots his chair closer to mine.
"Then you're not a geek. And neither am I.
We just like competition, is all."

"You're way too popular to be a geek,"
I tell him. And too gorgeous. He's wearing
a pricey-looking heather-green shirt that
makes the gold flecks in his eyes stand out,
and his jeans fit his body as well as they
would any gym-ripped Levi's model. "No

matter how smart you are or what kind of grades you get, your cool factor will always outweigh any geek tendencies. But when I was stressed out one afternoon last week, you know what I did? Worked ahead on Geometry. Get it? I used Geometry to relax."

He laughs aloud and runs his thumb along mine. I look down at our hands, and it puts my brain into hyper-spin. It's the whole thing I have for guys' hands.

I just have to STOP.

I start to glance up at the TV screens, but freeze when I see he's totally studying my face. "That's not geeky, Winslow, that's disturbed."

He's got a crooked smile as he says this, and I feel him pulling my chair closer to his with his foot. When I ask him what he's doing, keeping my voice light and jokey, he answers back, "I think you need a better way to relax."

Then he kisses me. Nothing too racy, but the promise of what he'd like to do later—when we're not in a crowded restaurant—is definitely there, messing with my mind enough for me to ignore his corny line about better ways to relax. (Did he get that from a movie, or what?)

He eases away, letting go of my hand a few seconds before the waitress comes to refill our sodas and ask if we're finished with our dinners. I don't even answer, I'm so distracted. I just let her take my plate.

A new trivia game starts, and David and I decide to defend our first-place finish. The couple at the bar's still there to give us a challenge, and a group of kids I vaguely recognize from Vienna West (I think they're seniors) are scooting into one of the booths with menus and a trivia pad. They keep looking at us. Probably wondering what Mr. Popular Smart Guy is doing out with the red-haired, pale-skinned goober girl.

We get the first question right, but don't get the second until they eliminate two answers, since we forget exactly how many men rode into the valley of death in Tennyson's "Charge of the Light Brigade" (six hundred). Then the third question pops onto the screen:

What's the capital of the European country of Schwerinborg?

A) Baden-Baden
B) Zurich
C) Freital
D) Interlaken

David cracks up beside me. "Well, I'm guessing you know this one. It's not Zurich, and I think Baden-Baden's in Germany, so it's either Interlaken or Freital . . . Freital, right?"

I nod, even though while he wasn't looking I went ahead and punched the button next to choice C. Of course we're the first ones to get it right, so we get the highest score on that question.

"Way to go, Winslow." He drapes one arm around the back of my chair. I don't object, but as he puts his hand on my back, tracing lines up and down, I start to get a funny feeling. Like something's wrong with this picture.

But what, I can't pinpoint. There aren't any reporters or photographers in here (because, being paranoid, I keep looking for them), and when I think about it, this actually fits my idea of a perfect date. Playing trivia games, talking about nothing in particular with a complete hottie who's, from all indications, totally into me. Being competitive without having to do it on a sports field, where I'm liable to get bashed and bruised. Hanging out and chatting and not feeling like we have to be anywhere at a certain time.

And the best part is that David really seems to like doing this too. Maybe, after dating super-popular types for so long, he's gotten sick of having to show up at all their parties and put on a show for their friends.

Maybe.

I try to shake the feeling something's off and just enjoy myself as we answer the next few questions. We're in second place, behind the seniors. I know it's them, because David says he's seen them playing here before, and they always use the same team name: MONSTER. In all caps. To make them extra scary or something, I suppose.

There's a break in the game, and a couple of the guys from the other table walk by on their way to the restroom and say hey to David.

"They're on the rugby team," he explains after they pass. "Well, some of them. I don't recognize the two guys on the end."

"Oh."

I look over and instantly get why I'm feeling so uncomfortable. The guys who are still in the booth are staring at me, trying to be as inconspicuous as possible while they either peek out from behind their menus or pretend they're watching basketball on the TV behind me.

All except for this one guy with long brown hair who's fidgeting with the plastic-encased menu that shows all the desserts. He puts it down and shoves his hair back from his face, and I realize it's John.

PFLAG John.

He's ditched the Kenny Chesney shirt for a navy blue NYU shirt that's actually kind of cool. But more than the shirt or the fact that his hair looks cleaner than the last time I saw him, it's his attitude that's setting off my inner alarms. The way he's intentionally not looking this way when all the other guys are.

Did he tell them about me? That my mom is gay? Is that why they keep looking over here?

I don't think we're supposed to talk about the stuff that comes up in meetings, and John didn't strike me as the type who *would* tell, even if there's no rule against it.

But if he did, will the rugby guys turn around and tell David?

Should I say something first? Make a pre-emptive strike?

Before I can decide, David (who's totally oblivious to the fact that the MONSTER guys are watching us) starts talking about what's going on at school—who's going out with whom and all the other gossip I've missed since I transferred. I'm interested, but I have a hard time keeping up because, on the inside, I'm totally freaked about what the rugby guys may or may not know. Then David gets off on a tangent talking about Christie and Jeremy and whether they've done it.

I know for certain they *haven't*. There hasn't even been any south-of-the-border action. But from the way David is talking, Jeremy hasn't confirmed the occurrence of full-blown sex one way or another to any of the guys, so they're all starting to make assumptions. Assumptions I know

Christie—who quietly prides herself on being a good Catholic girl—would not want them to make.

"So what about you, Val?" David asks.

"What about me what?"

"What do you think about the whole sex-before-marriage thing?"

"Why, you wanna do it on the table right now or something?" I try to sound funny instead of defensive, but I'm not sure I succeed. I mean, where did THAT question come from?

Guess I'm really more worried about David's opinions on sex between women at the moment.

Oh, ICK. I can't believe I just thought that.

He raises an eyebrow. "You making the invitation?"

I don't say anything (what can I possibly say?), and just grin like I made a big joke.

"Seriously, Winslow. Give me your ten-second opinion."

Is he trying to get me into bed? After, like, a date and a half?

"I don't have a problem with it." How

can I have a problem if it's never even come up? "The whole sex-before-marriage thing, that is. Not the sex here on the table thing. That, I cannot do. Sorry."

He laughs. "Same with me."

"Which part?"

"Both."

The way he says it makes me think he's testing me, though. Like there's a question behind his question.

"Why do you want to know?" Maybe I'm misreading the I-want-a-relationship vibe that's coming from him, which is usually different (or so Christie and Jules tell me) from the I-just-wanna-get-laid vibe. Besides, he can basically point to any of the girls in school and they'd be happy to give it up to him if all he wanted was a quickie hookup. No point in pursuing me, in that case.

"Well, I heard about that guy you've been seeing in Schwerinborg, and I just . . . I guess I wanted to know what your expectations would be if you decided you wanted to go out with me instead."

Come again? "I don't get it."

"Well, I imagine Prince Georg what's-his-name is the type who has certain expectations when he's going out with someone. Right?"

He's so *not* that kind of guy, but I'm not going to tell David that. I want to know his point. "And?"

"And you know what my father does for a living." He lowers his voice, as if he's embarrassed. Or worried someone might overhear. "I just can't—I can't risk doing anything that's going to reflect badly on him. So I wanted to let you know that up front. He's on Capitol Hill this week lobbying to take condoms out of public schools, since he thinks they encourage teenagers to have sex, and next week he has a meeting with two senators to discuss the gay marriage issue."

He reaches past me to punch the D button on the trivia pad, because while I was listening to him, a new question has popped up on the television screen.

He looks back at me. "It's not that I have a problem with condoms in schools. Or Christie and Jeremy doing whatever they do. Or even if you did it with that guy in Schwerinborg. I figure that's your business, you know?"

"I guess—"

"It's just that it's really important for my dad to be successful in his job. To encourage Congress to support President Carew and his policies, which will help him get re-elected. So I can't go around using the condoms from school, if you catch my meaning."

Uh-huh. "You're saying it'll undermine his work if anyone finds out. And the wrong people *always* find out."

"Exactly." He gives me a flirty grin, but I have no idea how to interpret it.

I can't believe I'm having *two* relationships where the guy's dad's job is a major impediment to my happiness. But Georg, who has a lot more pressure on him than David does, seems to handle it way better.

And it's pissing me off.

"So you think I'm here with you because I want to get busy? That's a pretty freaking big assumption you're making." Even if I have lusted after him for years and he knows it. (I'm guessing Jeremy's told him about my mondo crush, since I know Christie's told Jeremy.)

His face gets completely red. "That's

not what I'm saying. It's just that I like you a lot and I don't want you to think . . . well, I just want you to know where I'm coming from. I'm in kind of a weird position. Plus, my dad's trying to line me up with an internship in the Senate this summer. I can't ruin that opportunity."

He moves his hand up to play with my hair where it's hanging down my back. "But I don't want to ruin this opportunity either. Even if you are going back to Schwerinborg in a few days, I know you'll be back for good after the elections, right? At least, that's what Christie told Jeremy—that your dad plans to come back to the White House then."

"Well, it's not a firm plan or anything." I don't know why, but I feel like I shouldn't give him a straight answer. I mean, as far as I know, the whole Dad-returning-to-the-White-House thing isn't supposed to be public knowledge.

"So you understand?"

"Yeah." I understand better than he knows. It's like Georg, Take Two.

"So why did your dad leave the White House in the first place, if he's considering coming back after the election? There had to be a reason—something political, I'd guess—that might've made him want to leave for a while?"

He sounds totally casual about it, but I give him the Valerie Shrug. I'm not about to tell him my dad was temporarily "placed" with Prince Manfred because President Carew thought having an adviser going through a divorce from a lesbian could be an election-year liability.

I reach over to hit the A button on the trivia pad for *Michelangelo* (person who painted the ceiling in the Sistine Chapel), since—while I wasn't even paying attention—we moved into first place ahead of MONSTER, and now I don't want to lose the game.

I glance over at John. He's still not paying attention to me.

Once David and I answer the next question with *John Glenn*, I turn and ask him what's really on my mind: "So your dad's dealing with the gay-marriage issue next week?"

"Yeah."

I'm not even really sure how I feel

about it—I think I'll hurl if Mom gets married to Gabrielle, or anyone female—but I ask anyway. "What do you think about all that?"

"About gay marriage?" He glances sideways at me. "Why, are you for it?"

Okay, I cannot believe I'm having this discussion on, like, our second date. But since I kind of started it, I say, "I don't know. I haven't really thought about it—I'm not up on politics as much as you are. But I don't think someone who's gay should be discriminated against."

"It's not discrimination. It undermines the whole institution of marriage to allow gay couples to marry." He makes quotemarks in the air with his fingers as he says the word "marry." "I mean, where do you draw the line? What happens when these so-called married couples have kids? Will those kids grow up to marry the opposite sex? Will they think marriage is a joke?"

"A joke?"

He makes a face of disgust. "You bet. If gay marriage is legitimized, a hundred years from now marriage as we know it will cease to exist."

"I don't think that would happen." Geez, but this is a weird conversation. And freaking uncomfortable.

"Sure it will. Marriage wouldn't be valued anymore." He doesn't sound judgmental at all, just very matter-of-fact. "Think about it. We'd be changing thousands and thousands of years of history by legitimizing homosexuality. If we, as a nation, say that anyone can marry anyone else, man or woman, then what's special about marriage?"

Plenty, I want to tell him. But I don't. He sounds so sure of himself, and frankly, I'm not sure at all. About any of it.

And it's creeping me out to have PFLAG John only a few tables away while David and I are having this discussion.

"Hey," David says, taking his arm off the back of my chair and pointing to the screen, "I think we're about to win again. MONSTER missed that one entirely. Look!"

Sure enough, they did. The next question appears at the same time the waitress drops our check on the table. It's about Pickett's Charge, which we studied last semester in Mrs. Bennett's class.

David picks the correct answer, then gives me a killer smile that makes me want to ignore our entire discussion about gay marriage. How can he possibly be such a hottie and so smart but so set on ideas that maybe aren't so cut-and-dried?

"We make an awesome team, Winslow." He gives me another quick kiss before grabbing the bill.

Unfortunately, we miss the last trivia question—about an obscure 1960s football player—and end up in a tie with MONSTER. Probably for the best. I really don't want to tick them off.

After we put on our coats to leave, David pulls me over to their table. He introduces me, but instantly gets into a conversation about rugby. John looks up— since it'd be rude not to, I think—and he gives me a nod that lets me know he wants to say hello but that he's not going to acknowledge that he knows me. Or, at least, from where.

I give him a little smile of thanks when no one's looking. Then, when all the other guys start high-fiving one another over some big rugby play they made in their last game, he mouths, "No problem."

As grungy and strange as he is, I decide right then and there that John's a good guy.

But the something's-not-right-here feeling is still sticking in my gut, like I shouldn't be doing what I'm doing. But since we're about to leave, I force myself to ignore it.

After a few more minutes of rugby reminiscing, David puts his hand on my back and steers me out of TGI Friday's, since it's time for his brother and his brother's girlfriend to pick us up. David has them drop us off at the entrance to the apartment complex instead of at the door, so we can talk for a while as he walks me home.

And, I can tell, because he wants to kiss me again without his brother seeing. His brother gives us an *I know what you're doing* look, but I notice he's not exactly protesting having to wait for David. It gives him a few more minutes alone with his girlfriend—presumably to do the same thing.

As we start down the sidewalk, David grabs my hand. "I didn't want to say anything at dinner, but the guys at the other table were staring at you the whole time."

"Really?" So he did see.

"Yeah. One of them was trying to set me up with a friend of his, and I told them I couldn't—that someone I really liked was coming to town and that I thought I might be otherwise occupied."

"Oh."

"I just wanted to tell you in case you were wondering why they were staring. They were probably curious."

We get to one of the darker places on the sidewalk, in between the glow of two streetlights, and he stops walking and pulls me right into his arms. "Thanks for keeping me otherwise occupied."

I let him kiss me. This time, since we're alone, it's finally a real kiss.

And after all these years of dreaming about it—of dying every time he looked at me or slowed down on the walk to school so I could catch up to him and his friends—the whole kissing-David thing just doesn't do it for me.

"You're the best, you know that, Valerie?"

"Thanks." I want him not to say any more. It's making me feel horrid.

"I always thought we'd be good together, you know? I kind of suspected you might have a thing for me, but I didn't know for sure until Christie told me a few weeks ago."

The blessing of a friend with a big mouth. At least she didn't tell him I've wanted him like mad since I was five. Geez, I hope she had that much sense.

"But I was stupid, and I never did anything about it." He twists a few strands of my hair around his finger, then lets go and starts running his hand along my shoulder. "I kept asking out other girls, thinking that they were what I wanted."

Yeah, the future prom queen types. Who wouldn't want them?

"So why me?" I ask, even though I'm not sure I really want to know.

"I think it took hearing you were going away to realize that, in the end, all I've wanted is someone who thinks like I do. And Winslow, I believe you're it."

Hoo, boy. If he only knew.

I let him give me a few more quick

kisses, then say, "I think your brother's waiting."

"I doubt it. But I don't want you to miss your curfew." He walks me to the door and says he'll call me—he wants to see me as much as possible before I have to go back to Schwerinborg.

I thank him for dinner and trivia, then duck in the door. As I watch him walk back toward his brother's car from the glass windows of the stairwell, I feel tears burning up in my eyes. After they drive away, I sit down on the stairs.

I realize that I want the same thing David does: Someone who thinks like me. Or, more accurately, someone who gets me. Who doesn't just spout his opinion and expect that I'll agree. Someone who will listen to and respect my opinion, too, even if he doesn't agree.

Someone who won't expect me to be his Armor Girl.

I let myself into the apartment as quietly as possible. Mom left on the reading light in the living room, but it looks like she's gone to bed.

Good thing, because I know she'd want to talk. And I need time to digest what has happened.

Maybe I'll make a list. David in one column, Georg in the other. Just to be certain. Although, in my gut, I know what the answer will be.

No. Too *Glamour* magazine. Although it did help when I did it at the PFLAG meeting, so maybe—

"What's wrong, honey?"

I jump about a mile. What's she doing lurking in the kitchen without the light on? "Geez, Mom! You scared the crap outta me!"

"Sorry. I was just getting a glass of milk," she says, holding it up as proof. "I was reading in the living room, waiting for you to get home."

Of course she was.

"You look upset. Did something bad happen on your date?"

"No, we had a good time." At least, until I woke up to reality. And now I feel horrible. I should never, never have gone out with David tonight. Going to the movies was one thing. That was supposedly casual. A favor to Christie, sort of, and because I'd committed to it when I thought Georg and I might still be "cooling off," even though apparently he never meant it that way.

But tonight—tonight was a massive, no, make that a monster (ha-ha), mistake. Because if I'd taken a fraction of a second to think about it, I'd have known I wanted Georg, not David. And I never would have sent him that e-mail telling him I'd meet him.

Why did I do that??

Why did I not realize that's the reason I felt wrong all night? I should have been here, either thinking about Georg or hanging with the girls. Doing anything except going out with David.

"You don't look like you had a good time, Valerie. You look disturbed."

"I don't want to talk about it, Mom."

"Okay. But it might help to get it off your chest." She walks past me and picks up her book—the latest best seller by one of Oprah's self-help gurus—from the end table and gives me one of her *I'm an understanding mom* looks before sitting down.

"And Gabrielle's not here. She went out to dinner with some of her friends from Weight Watchers after their meeting tonight."

"So they can pig out on pizza?"

Parallel lines of disapproval appear between Mom's eyes. "Valerie—"

"I'm *kidding*. I know Gabrielle takes it seriously."

Mom just stares at me. Doesn't start reading her book, doesn't give me the usual spiel about how Gabby lost a ton of weight a couple years ago with the program, and how she now feels she owes her low cholesterol levels and "Earth-friendly" vegan lifestyle to the good folks at Weight Watchers.

Clearly she's not going anywhere until I spill about my date. But I just can't.

I feel too rotten to talk to anyone, let alone my mother. I mean, what does *she* know about staying loyal to someone?

I toss my purse on the counter because I know she's not going to let me go to bed. And I don't know that I can sleep, anyway. "Mom, stop staring at me."

"No, I don't think I will."

Fine. Two can play this game. I put my hands on my hips. "Okay, then answer a question for me. Did you cheat on Dad?"

Ten

I let my hands fall to my side.

Where in the world did *that* come from? What is *wrong* with me? The way I'm acting tonight, I have to wonder which circle of hell I'm destined to occupy.

"I'm so sorry, Mom, it's totally none of my—"

"I didn't cheat on your father. Nothing happened with Gabrielle until after I told you and your father I wanted a divorce." She takes a deep breath and fiddles with the ties on the front of her robe until they're pulled tight. "Is that what you're upset about?"

Wow. This was so *not* the answer I

expected to hear. "You didn't cheat?"

"No." She doesn't look the least bit uncomfortable with this topic—when, if our roles were reversed, I'd kill me for asking—so I figure she's been planning her answer for a long time. "But when I met Gabrielle, I knew. Sometimes, you *just know.* In here." She taps her chest as she talks. "And it woke me up. I realized that I wanted Gabrielle in my life, most likely for the rest of my life, and to pursue that, I needed to leave your father first."

"How did you know Gabrielle would want you?"

This draws a smile out of her. "I had my suspicions. Well, they were more than suspicions, I suppose. She'd been flirting with me a little, and me with her. But neither one of us acted on our attraction—we never even spoke of it—because I was married. But even if she'd never flirted, I knew that I couldn't be with your father anymore. Staying with him when I felt that way about someone else—anyone else—would be cheating both myself and him. And you, too. I've always wanted you to be true to yourself, and if I lived a lie, what kind of example would I be to you? How could you respect me if I couldn't respect myself?"

She lets out a little sigh, then continues. "So before things got out of hand, I told Gabrielle how I felt about her, and that whether she returned my feelings or not, I'd decided to leave your father that night. It was a huge, huge risk for me to do that. Not just emotionally, but financially, too, because I knew leaving your father also meant I'd have to go back to teaching. And I wasn't sure I could do that and enjoy it."

I am beyond stunned. I just cannot picture my mom having all this angst and my never even realizing it. Ignoring the teaching thing for the moment, I say, "But Gabrielle returned your feelings?"

Mom nodded. "She said she had fallen in love with me, and that she wanted us to be together. She just knew the same way I knew that we belonged together, and for the long term. But, again, neither Gabrielle nor I acted until *after* I came home and told you and your dad. It would have cast a pall on our relationship to have taken that first step physically before I'd ended things with your father. And Gabby and I wanted to start clean."

Wow. She sounds like she's been reading waaaay too many self-help books (probably because she has been), but still . . . I never realized how hard all this has been for her. And how much she worried about what *I* might think.

I cross the room and sit on the arm of the chair next to hers. "So you didn't *just know* with Dad? Before you married him?"

She gives me a sad little smile and wraps one of the ties to her robe around her wrist, then unwraps it. "I wanted your father to be the love of my life. I really did. I wanted a nice life in the suburbs with kids and the whole shebang."

"But . . . ?"

"But no, there was never any lightning bolt, *aha* kind of moment. I always had fun with your father—I liked him a lot, and will always love him on some level—but I know in my heart that I'm attracted to women and I'm just not capable of loving any man the way I should." She takes a long drink of her milk, then sets it on top of the Oprah book on the end table.

"I just wish I'd been honest with myself about it sooner," she adds. "I could have saved us all a lot of pain."

"But then you wouldn't have had me. *I* wouldn't even have me."

Her face splits into a wide grin at this. "No, and I don't know what I would have done without you."

"I'm sorry I thought you were cheating," I tell her. "I should have known better." I think.

"It's all right. I figured you'd have questions after you went to the PFLAG meeting. That's why I've stayed up late the last couple nights, so you could talk to me if you wanted to. You're not here long, and I wanted to make the most of our time."

"Well, I'm not asking because of PFLAG. I'm asking because of me. I-I feel like I'm cheating, and I guess I needed advice." I wave my hand in front of me, as if I can erase the words from the air. "That just came out all wrong. I'm not saying that—"

She frowns. "How, exactly, do you think *you're* cheating?"

So I flop backward into the chair and tell her everything. Well, not everything.

But I do tell her about Georg's "cool off" call, and then the e-mail from Zermatt, and how I went out with David, anyway—that the first time was theoretically casual, even though I let him hold my hand in the theater and I could have pulled away and just stopped everything right there. But then I was even worse and went out with David a second time. Where it was just the two of us, and it was definitely a date.

And I tell her that now I feel like I'm being one of those evil, bitchy types of girls who cheat on their boyfriends, and that's just beyond wrong.

"Valerie, how old are you?"

"Um, Mom, you should know."

"Fifteen, honey. *Fifteen.* And, to my knowledge, you and Georg aren't married."

"Not to my knowledge either."

"And you made no promises to each other. So you're not cheating—in fact, you're perfectly normal. You and Georg have only been together a short time, Valerie. Far too short a time to be committed, even though the connection you felt with him sounds pretty intense."

Intense? "Mom, don't try to sound cool."

"I'm not. I'm just trying to get it through your head that you're doing the right thing. Think—what if I'd taken the time to date around, to make sure your father was really the right guy for me? What if I'd taken the time to be certain about my decision? That's all you're doing."

"So going out with David was a good thing?"

She grins and reaches over to grab my foot where it's hanging over the side of the armchair, then gives it a little shake, exactly the way Dad does. "Yes. It sounds like you've learned what you don't want, at least for now. And in many cases, learning what you don't want is as important as learning what you do want. Or *who* you want."

"I think I know who I want."

"For now." She lets go of my foot. "Remember—you're fifteen. You have plenty of time to learn as much as you can—about Georg, about other boys. About yourself. Use that time wisely."

I must still look uncertain, because as she stands up to go to bed, she says, "And trust in your friends. Jules and Natalie will understand. And so will Christie. Make the choices that are best for you, not the choices you think will please them."

As she walks down the hall, I say to her back, "I don't know what you're thinking about teaching, Mom, but if you do go back, you're going to be great."

She stops, looks back at me, and says, "You know, I think I will. I wasn't ready when I was young. Now I'm looking forward to it." Her face splits into a big grin, and she adds, "Proves my point that it takes a while to learn what you really want in life."

To: Val@viennawest.edu
From: ChristieT@viennawest.edu
Subject: David, of course

WELL?!?

To: ChristieT@viennawest.edu
From: Val@viennawest.edu
Subject: RE: David, of course

WELL . . . it went well. We played trivia, we

acted like the total geeks we are, we had a good time.

But—and please, please, do not kill me for saying this—as great as David and I get along, and as much as we have in common, I don't think there's a spark.

No cosmic connection, no yo-baby-do-I-belong-with-this-guy. Nothing like what you have with Jeremy.

In my gut, I still believe I'm David's Armor Girl. It just took going out with him a couple of times to know it for sure.

And, in many ways, maybe he's my Armor Guy. Someone I can enjoy being around, someone who gets along with my friends and who looks fantabulous and says all the right things to everyone.

But he's not THE guy.

I promised to tell you the truth from now on, so there it is.

I'm really sorry!!

Of course, now I have to figure out what to say if (when) he asks me out again. I already have e-mail from him . . . opening that one next. . . .

Val

To: Val@viennawest.edu
From: RugbyDave@viennawest.edu
Subject: Last night

Hey Valerie-who-is-also-Val,

   Did we rock on trivia last night or what? Want to do it again before you leave, just so we can prove our utter geekiness?

   Or—a bunch of the rugby guys are getting together at this guy Kevin's house for a party the day before you leave. Might be fun.

   Later,
   David-not-Dave

To: RugbyDave@viennawest.edu
From: Val@viennawest.edu
Subject: RE: Last night

David-not-Dave,

   One: Yes, we did, indeed, rock on trivia. Did you expect any less than us dominating the entire TGI Friday's crowd?

   Two: While I'd love to do it again, I can't. Well, more accurately, I think it'd be a bad idea. I really do like you a lot—just ask Christie, since you know she's painfully honest about everything—but my life is in a chaotic mess right now, and I don't want to lead you on. I just can't do the whole relationship thing.

Three: I really am very, very sorry. You do know you're pretty much the hottest guy in school, right? And that you should NOT take this personally?

I'm sure I'm messing this up, and should probably do this in person, but I am a wuss. Please forgive me?

Valerie-who-is-also-Val

To: Val@viennawest.edu
From: RugbyDave@viennawest.edu
Subject: Valerie Winslow ((Attachment: valemail.doc)

Jeremy,

I must've blown it, man. She thinks I'm a "bad idea" (I've attached the e-mail she sent me.) If it wasn't for my dad getting on my case about everything, I'd just tell her to bite me.

Whatever. Maybe I'll see if Melanie Fergusson wants to come to the rugby party.

David

To: Val@viennawest.edu
From: RugbyDave@viennawest.edu

Subject: BIG mistake . . .

Okay——huge apology. I meant to send that to Jeremy. I accidentally hit Reply instead of Forward.

And even then . . . you know I would never tell you to bite me (no matter what my dad says), so please, please, forgive me. I was suffering from Temporary Pissed-Offedness.

And I do forgive you. So I hope that makes us even. Friends?

David

To: RugbyDave@viennawest.edu
From: Val@viennawest.edu
Subject: RE: BIG mistake . . .

Yes, friends. And you can tell me to bite you if you feel the need (but don't expect me to actually do it!). Consider Temporary Pissed-Offedness as a total defense.

Besides—I'd hate to have to play against you in trivia when I get home from Schwerinborg for good. I'd much rather you were on my team.

Val

To: Val@viennawest.edu
From: ChristieT@viennawest.edu
Subject: LOL!!

Oh. WOW. That e-mail exchange between you and David was TOO TOO FUNNY. (Yes, David forwarded it all to Jeremy, who forwarded to me.)

I already forgive you for not going out with him again. Even temporary anger is no reason for a guy to say "bite me" to YOU. Really. You are the coolest person on Earth.

AND . . . I just got the newest Orlando Bloom flick on DVD. Want to come over? My mom says she can pick you up. We can talk about David and Jeremy and your mom and whatever else you want. I've missed you so much!!

See you in an hour?

Love,

Christie

P.S.: Jules thinks you should walk up to David next time you see him and actually bite him.

P.P.S.: Natalie says she will not make any comments regarding violence one way or another until she is out of the maximum security block or the prison guards might not recommend her for parole.

The pilot's voice comes over the intercom, waking up half the people on the flight. We're starting our descent into Munich, so he says anyone who wants to go to the restroom should either go now or hold it until we land in Germany.

I glance at my watch, then back at the huge screen covering the wall at the front of coach class. It alternately flashes a map showing the plane's location over Europe with a list of our airspeed, altitude, and the distance to Munich.

I've been watching it count down the miles (and kilometers) ever since the inflight movie ended an hour ago. Thankfully, we're on time and I won't miss my connection to Freital, because I cannot wait to get there. Dad will be waiting, and he says we're going straight back to the palace because he has to work today. Prince Manfred's hosting the president of Taiwan tonight, so Dad needs to do his protocol thing.

Fine by me. The sooner I get to the palace, the better.

I glance down at the piece of paper on

the tray table in front of me. I read nearly all of the *Is Homosexuality a Sin?* book, though I was getting some strange looks from other passengers and I finally put it away, figuring it'd be better to read the rest at home. Sometime when Dad's not around.

So to kill time, I started making a list. Just to help me see everything in black and white.

David Anderson
• *Driven to do well in school (like me)*
• *Has lots of the same friends I do*
• *I've known him forever*
• *Good-hearted and polite*
• *The body. The hands. The eyes.*
• *CONS: Anti-gay. Is careful with his behavior because of his dad's job.*

Georg
• *More adventurous than me, in a good way*
• *Good-hearted and polite*
• *The body. The hands. The eyes. The arms. The ACCENT.*
• *CONS: The press office wants to*

sanction our every move. Is careful
with his behavior because of his dad's
job.

Georg's list is way shorter than David's, probably because David and I have so much in common. Their cons are similar—they both have dads whose jobs change how they have to act when they're with their girlfriends.

Except Georg doesn't have the major cons that David has. Georg doesn't care about my mom's lifestyle. And even though he's someday going to have his father's job (like I suspect David will also have, or something like it), he doesn't let it change his everyday behavior or who he is on the inside.

And he doesn't let it change what he feels about me.

I crumple up the list, push up my tray table, then yank the airsick bag out of the seat pocket and stuff the list inside. I glance toward the back of the plane, and since there's no line, I unbuckle, walk to the miniscule airplane lavatory, and push the airsick bag through the trash slot.

In exactly fifty-three minutes, the plane will land and nothing I wrote on paper matters. All that matters is that I'm DYING to see a certain prince named Georg Jacques von Ederhollern. Even if I have to sneak out of the palace apartment to do it.

I want to be his princess.

I cannot believe it. No Dad. Anywhere.

I scan the entire area where passengers exit the security gate, but no luck. A half-dozen or so people are dressed in black outfits, holding their driving hats and clutching signs bearing the last names of passengers other than me. Otherwise, it's pretty darned empty.

The plane from Munich to Freital ended up ten minutes late due to the perpetual rain in this country, so even if Dad was running behind, which he never is, he should definitely be here.

I walk across the open area of the terminal to this huge wall of television screens showing arrival and departure information. Yep, they got my flight correct. It shows us right there in green, and says this is the proper terminal for meeting passengers. Even though it's all in German, I can understand that much.

"Excuse me," a low voice says next to me. Since most people flying into Freital speak various European languages, I'm wondering how this person can possibly pinpoint me as American. But then I take a good look at the guy—who's wearing a baseball cap pulled low over his forehead—and drop my duffel bag on the ground.

"Georg!"

"Shhh!" He grins at me, then looks over his shoulder toward the passengers from my flight as they filter through the security gate to meet up with their rides. "I had to see you, so I talked your father into letting me come along."

"Where is he?"

"Baggage claim."

"Oh. Thanks." I want to hug him right there, but I'm not absolutely positive where things stand.

"I think I made a huge mistake," he says. "When I called you and said we had to cool it, I didn't call back or e-mail you to explain."

"That's okay."

"No, it's not." He looks at the floor while a young French-ish-looking couple with backpacks slung over their shoulders walks past us. "My parents were all on my case." He frowns, then asks, "Is that how you say it? 'On my case'?"

I think the smile on my face must be the dorkiest ever, but the way he always has to ask me about his English is *soooo* delicious. "Yes, that's it."

"Well, they were all on my case about the newspaper article, and telling me I had to call you that instant to make certain we weren't seen together in public for a while, and all the press guys were in our apartment, discussing it with my father, and I caved."

"I understand."

He lets out an exasperated grunt. "It's fine for us to keep things cool in public if we need to, but it's not fine for you to think I don't want to be with you. Because I do. And I told my parents that when I got home from Zermatt."

He picks up my duffel bag and loops it over his shoulder, then reaches for my hand with his free one and leads me toward the escalator to baggage claim.

"I think the cold air on the ski slopes cleared my brain," he says as we descend. "I couldn't stop thinking about you—about how funny you are, or about how you tell me what you think and not just what I want to hear. And I kept thinking about our night in the garden, and how much I like hanging out with you and just talking. And I realized we belong together—and if we really want this, we'll find a way to make it work. I just hope you feel the same."

My heart is thumping about a hundred miles an hour as we step off the escalator toward the rows of baggage claim carousels.

Man, do I want him. Bad. And not just for long, slow kisses. For everything—walking to school, talking about the world, laughing at each other. Every freaking thing.

"But what about the reporters?" I look at the faces of the people passing through baggage claim—mostly dour-looking Europeans my parents' age juggling their suitcases, trying to figure out how to find the taxi stand or the parking garage. "Didn't your parents freak when you told them you were coming to the airport?"

"I promised to keep a low profile. But I had to see you. And what can reporters possibly say or photograph if your father is with us?"

"Or if you're in that baseball hat," I tease him. "You know you've gotta lose that. You're not the baseball hat type."

"Great. But you're not answering my question," he says.

"Which one?"

"Do you still want to be with me?"

I try to give him a serious look, like I have to think it over, but I just can't. I'm giddy-happy-scary in love with the guy—even more than before spin control happened—and every second I wait to tell him is killing me.

Who knew going out with David would actually strengthen what I feel for Georg?

I tilt my head so I can see into his eyes despite the silly baseball hat. "What if I told you I really want to kiss you like you've never been kissed before? Right here, right now, in the middle of the

Lufthansa Airlines baggage claim?"

"Please don't."

I spin at the hissed words coming from behind me in a way-too-familiar voice. "Um, Dad. Hi."

"Hi, yourself." He has a welcoming sort of smile on his face, so I hope that means I haven't made him mad by wanting to jump Georg—especially given the fact I'm supposed to be controlling spin. "I have a car waiting at the curb, if you can hold off on your plans for about two minutes. This is a public area, you realize."

I can feel myself turning bright red all the way to my ears. There are certain things a father is just not supposed to hear.

"Thank you, Mr. Winslow," Georg says, sounding all princely and polite despite his casual clothes.

When we get to the car—a black Mercedes with tinted windows that, believe it or not, doesn't stick out in Schwerinborg, since everyone here drives high-end European cars—I realize that Dad is driving. No one else from the palace came.

"You guys really are trying to be discreet," I say to Georg as I look around for reporters lurking curbside, but see none.

"Just get in," Dad says, so I do.

I cannot freaking believe it. Dad and Georg have McDonald's for me. And a huge bouquet of flowers. All of it's in the middle of the backseat.

"I figured you've been eating Gabrielle's vegan food all week," Georg explains.

"You're bribing me?"

"Whatever it takes."

As we pull out into traffic, heading away from the airport, he leans across the seat (well, as far as his seat belt will allow, since Dad's a stickler for seat belts), puts his hands on my cheeks, and pulls me toward him for a major mind-blowing kiss.

"Ahem. This isn't a limo. There's no privacy panel."

"Sorry, Mr. Winslow," Georg says. He leans back in his seat and winks at me, making me feel completely warm inside despite the drizzle hitting the windshield and the gray Schwerinborg skies. Then, just so I'm completely happy, he opens the Mickey D's bag and hands me the fries, which smell absolutely decadent.

"Fortification against Steffi," he says. "Though I think we'll be able to deal with her better now. Ulrike's on our side, too, since you left."

I see my dad grin to himself in the rearview mirror.

"That's something." Though I couldn't care less about the girls at school right now. All I can think about is Georg. I offer him a few of my fries, but he waves them off. Instead, he reaches back into the bag and offers me my favorite—a McChicken. And it's fixed just the way I like it.

"True love," Georg mouths to me.

I think I'm going to cry, but I manage to hold it in long enough to smile and mouth back, "I love you, too."

Because I do. I just know.

The books that all your mates have been talking about!

Collect all the books in the best-selling series by

Cathy Hopkins

"Bridget Jones as a Teen"

—Teen People